Three Original Screenplays

SUN MOON AND THREE LESS STARS

CALEZE

Lolana Mack Publishing

ISBN:978-0-9977804-7-5

Published by: Lolana Mack Publishing

(lolanamackpublishing@gmail.com)

Layout:Muhammad

Images and Drawings: Caleze

Cover Design: Caleze and Janiel Escueta

For

Irene S. Funderburg

TABLE OF CONTENT

THE SEED

The seed can't grow without the dirt

The dirt represents life, which could be full of hurt

The sun will shine upon that covered **seed**

A kind word every now and then will forever feed

Inside the ground all dark and alone

It feels as if you have been stripped to the bone

The rain will penetrate the seed's hard shell

It will allow growth the seed will tell

A life **will** spring from a dirt-covered seed

Remember to pray to choke off the weeds

The seed will grow if you allow the change

Don't let the darkness make you feel so strange

The root will stretch and grab to the soil

SUN MOON AND THREE LESS STARS

Before you know it, the seed did not spoil

The leaves will **bring** forth a fresh new life

You thought the dirt just represented strife

The seed, a planted word each and everyday

Now what have you planted as you let **life** pass by your way?

The seed, Remember the seed.

THE LAW OF FREEMAN

THE LAW OF FREE MAN

written by

Caleze

What is "MAN"?

INT. JAMIE'S APARTMENT - LIVING ROOM - DAY - MODERN DAY

A father and son - DR. ABRAHAM RICHARDSON and JAMIE RICHARDSON - lock eyes in battle.

ABRAHAM, 46, mild-mannered, salt and pepper beard, a scientist/pipe-smoker look, is dressed in reading glasses, a denim dress shirt, a cardigan and slacks.

JAMIE, 22, carefree, young man with the wild haired model look, is dressed in reading glasses, a white t-shirt, blue jeans and sneakers.

They sit in a barely furnished living room, Abraham leaned back in an accent chair and Jamie slouched into a loveseat. Neither ready to speak first. Abraham shifts his weight to the edge of the seat and sighs with a great force.

ABRAHAM

I feel as though I've done you a disservice.

Nothing.

ABRAHAM (CONT'D)

All this time I've given you a lot of leeway in hopes that you would finally find your own footing.

Jamie slouches and drops deeper into the seat, his face now bubbling with aggression.

ABRAHAM (CONT'D)

All of the things. All of the things I have done for you. Your lifestyle, your apartment... that!

Abraham points to the ankle monitor on Jamie. Jamie crosses his arms and sits up some, never looking at Abraham.

JAMIE

You've always wanted me to be YOU so badly. I can't! I just can't! You go out and become a doctor, you get your own company, you leave me with mom forever and then expect me to turn out like what? Like you?

(scoff) Please!

Abraham's eyes water, he sits for a moment. Jamie still won't make eye contact. He's busy staring at a statue on the tv ledge, a wolf with a lamb in its mouth.

ABRAHAM

(leaning in)

No... I wanted you to be better than me.

Silence. Both males sit without a word as their thoughts permeate. Abraham drops his head and fiddles with his wedding ring.

ABRAHAM (CONT'D)

I tried to be better to you. Anything you wanted. You could have it. Money. Connections. Attention. My own literal heart if necessary. And yet... you don't appreciate it because you haven't had to go without. You haven't had to scrape what little you had together to make it work, and for that I am truly sorry, son.

Abraham stands and slowly walks to the front door.

ABRAHAM (CONT'D)

(facing the door)

Maybe this will help you grow up.

Abraham exits the apartment, a gust of energy leaving with him. Jamie violently sniffs and wipes a tear from his eye. His new ankle jewelry stealing his gaze as reality hits him.

DISSOLVE TO:

INT. JAMIE'S APARTMENT - BEDROOM - DAY

A room so clean and well organized, you could use it alone to sell the apartment. Jamie sits in a rolling office chair between the window and his bed. A tablet in his lap, watching fight videos. His phone sitting on the bed beside him, face up. The phone BUZZES and lights up with a Text Message from "Rough Riders *American Flag Emoji*". Jamie picks up the phone and opens the group chat with TEDDY, LEON and PETER.

TEDDY (TEXT)

"Bro... you good?"

LEON (TEXT)

"Yeah, how'd it go?"

Jamie types back.

JAMIE (TEXT)

"Yeah, my dad got me house arrest"

Jamie sits his phone down but doesn't turn it off. Soon, another message pops up.

TEDDY (TEXT)

"That's good right? You almost got a few years"

Before Jamie can type back...

PETER (TEXT)

"Do you tell them"

Jamie's face scrunches and he tilts his head.

JAMIE

(out loud)

The hell does that even mean?

Teddy and Leon text back immediately.

LEON (TEXT)

"Huh?"

TEDDY (TEXT)

"Tf are you saying?"

PETER (TEXT)

"My bad I meant did you tell them about us? The police"

JAMIE (TEXT)

"Are you guys on house arrest too?"

"No"

PETER (TEXT)

JAMIE (TEXT)

(with attitude)

"Then obviously not"

LEON (TEXT)

"Peter... *face palm emoji*"

PETER (TEXT)

"I had to ask"

TEDDY (TEXT)

"You didn't but anyway... how long did you get Jamie?"

Jamie sighs and hesitates before responding.

JAMIE (TEXT)

"I got a year..."

TEDDY (TEXT)

"Shit bro I'm sorry"

Jamie speaks to himself.

JAMIE

Of course, you are.

TEDDY (TEXT)

"Maybe they let you off early"

Jamie scoffs, then types back.

JAMIE (TEXT)

"For what we did? Never!"

TEDDY (TEXT)

"Hey who knows? Never say never"

Jamie leans back in his chair and tosses his phone back on the bed.

JAMIE

"Never say never", huh? Gimme a break.

He plops the tablet down on the bed also, then lays his head back and massages his face.

INSERT - TEXT MESSAGE

The phone illuminates and another text from Teddy drops down. "I guess we'll have to go out without you tonight"

With a puff of disappointment, Jamie trembles violently. His blood boiling as he looks right at us with destruction in his eyes.

JAMIE (V.O.)

That little bastard thinks he can take my place. He always wanted to lead so bad, and I just handed it to him on a silver fucking platter. Why didn't you just rat those leaches out. The three of them put together wouldn't make up half the man you are. Maybe... just maybe you should have sold them out. You could find ten more just like them. Those bastards. I'll show them.

(MORE)

JAMIE (V.O.) (CONT'D)

I'll do this time and then come back even more dominant. They'll bend or they'll break, but one way or the other I'll get my spot back. I'll make them beg me to get out of their asses. Then, they'll remember a true Alpha when they see me again.

A smirk glides across Jamie's face as he relaxes and leans back into his chair, putting his feet up on the bed, hands behind his head.

INT. JAMIE'S APARTMENT - BEDROOM - DAY - MONTAGE

- Jamie does push-ups
- Jamie does pull-ups on his doorway rack
- The phone illuminates to show "Leon has posted"
- Jamie does squats, ignoring the phone
- The phone illuminates to show "Peter has posted"
- Jamie picks the phone up and watches the videos of his drunk friends partying
- Jamie does push-ups harder and faster
- Jamie does pull-ups harder, sweat flying
- Jamie does sit-ups until he finally gasses out

INT. JAMIE'S APARTMENT - BATHROOM - MOMENTS LATER

Jamie walks into his bathroom, drops his toilet lid and sits on it. His breathing labored and clothes soaked.

QUICK FLASH

A group of guys flailing around. BACK TO SCENE

QUICK FLASH

A girl screaming. BACK TO SCENE QUICK FLASH

A guy on top of the girl screaming. BACK TO SCENE

Jamie trembles and looks down to a growing bulge in his shorts.

DISSOLVE TO:

INT. JAMIE'S APARTMENT - BEDROOM - DAY

Jamie sits on the edge of his bed, masturbating with force. He grunts and shifts repeatedly as he tries to get off. His phone - a video playing - in one hand, his appendage in the other.

INT. JAMIE'S APARTMENT - LIVING ROOM - NIGHT

The TV is on an animal network. Jamie lies across his sofa, his eyes getting weaker as he doses off.

INSERT - NATURE SHOW

A pack of light-colored wolves chase and hunt elk in a snowy terrain. Suddenly, the Alpha wolf gets separated from his pack. As he runs through the snow, another wolf stalks him. This one much larger and black-colored with a meanness about him. Just as the smaller wolf notices the larger, it's too late as he's already...

BACK TO SCENE

KNOCK KNOCK KNOCK!!! Jamie is startled as something beats on the door. He's slow to make his way to the door. Jamie slides his eye to the peephole, and nobody is there. He walks back to his sofa.

JAMIE

Stupid ding-dong ditching.

Just as Jamie sits, his phone VIBRATES in his pocket.

Jamie spreads his body out across the sofa face down and looks at the phone deliriously - "No Caller ID". He answers the phone and slides it to his ear. A black man who sounds as if he's codeswitching - CHARLIE - responds on the other end.

JAMIE (CONT'D)

Hello?

CHARLIE (V.O.)

Hello, this is Charlie from Recession Restoration. I would like to know if you are interested in upgrading your hair loss prevention program?

Jamie "wakes up" and smacks his teeth. He then ends the call. Just as he sits up, the phone VIBRATES again. He answers it again.

CHARLIE (V.O.) (CONT'D)

Hello, Jamie are you there?

JAMIE

Yo, what the hell do you want?

CHARLIE (V.O.)

Well sir, as I said, "I would like to know if you would like to upgrade your hair loss prevention?".

JAMIE

I'm too young to have hair loss!

CHARLIE (V.O.)

Are you?

Charlie shuffles through some papers on his side of the phone.

CHARLIE (V.O.) (CONT'D)

I see.

(invitingly)

Well then, it's always a great time to start!

Jamie drags his hand down his face in anger and sighs deeply as he bubbles over.

JAMIE

Fuck you! Fuck your hair loss prevention! Fuck your stupid ass proper voice! Fuck this day! Fuck off! Don't call back, you prick!

Jamie hangs up his phone.

BLACK SCREEN:

SUPER: "Three Months Later"

DISSOLVE TO:

EXT. JAMIE'S APARTMENT - BALCONY - NIGHT

Jamie stands on his balcony, looking over the street. He's lost a considerable amount of weight and grown out the little facial hair he can. His hair wilder than ever and his eyes baggy. He inhales deeply, then walks back inside.

INT. JAMIE'S APARTMENT - LIVING ROOM - CONTINUOUS

Jamie walks in and immediately slouches down into the corner of a living room wall. He pulls out his phone, swipes through it and taps the contact "Dad". Abraham's number goes to voicemail.

ABRAHAM (V.O.)

Good day, this is Dr. Abraham Richardson. I apologize for missing your call, but if you would please leave your name, number and a brief message, I will get back to you as soon as possible. Have a marvelous day.

MESSAGE DING. Jamie sits for a while before speaking.

JAMIE

You "apologize"? You "apologize for missing my call"? It's been months. You're just gonna let your son starve, huh? You're fine with that? That help you sleep at night?

Knowing I'm on my last leg... knowing I can't do it alone? You just want me to beg you, but I won't. I'm gonna make it out of this on my own and then you'll see.

Hangs up the phone and drops it to the ground. Jamie stares at his torn socks for a few moments - KNOCK KNOCK - somebody knocks on the door. There's a hesitation before he even gets up from the floor. As he stands and walks closer to the door, he takes his time almost as if he's counting his steps. He walks out of the office, through the living room and to the door.

KNOCK KNOCK.

The knocks get even harder this time. Jamie slides his hand over the peephole and yells...

JAMIE (CONT'D)

Who is it!

No response.

JAMIE (CONT'D)

(timidly)

Yo if you don't speak I ain't gonna open it!

Still no response. A few seconds pass as... KNOCK KNOCK KNOCK KNOCK KNOCK...

The rapid-paced beating startles Jamie so badly his knees almost give out. He takes a deep breath and then... just as he's about to open the door, it gets kicked open. Narrowly missing Jamie, the door slams a dent into the wall.

JAMIE (CONT'D)

What the fuck, man!

EXT. JAMIE'S APARTMENT - DOORWAY - CONTINUOUS

Nothing. Jamie looks around the frame, but nobody is outside the door. Jamie pokes his head out and surveys the community. Just cars and plants as far as can be seen.

JAMIE

Yeah, you better run before I get here! Better be glad I didn't have my gun, or you'd be dead!

He slams the door.

INT. JAMIE'S APARTMENT - LIVING ROOM - MOMENTS LATER

As Jamie walks in, the NEIGHBOR upstairs begins stomping and yelling through the ceiling.

NEIGHBOR (V.O.)

Quiet down, you dick!

Jamie walks over and slams himself down into the sofa. He's slouched so deeply he's almost folded. Jamie exhales deeply and lays his head back to stare at the ceiling.

INT. JAMIE'S BEDROOM - NIGHT

We come in on the phone, Jamie in the background getting ready for bed. The phone VIBRATES and shows "No Caller ID". Jamie makes his way over and hesitates as he reads the name... or lack thereof. He finally swipes to answer the call. A MAN answers in a charming and refined Spanish accent.

MAN (V.O.)

Señor Jamie? How are you on this fine day?

JAMIE

Who is this?

The Man chuckles and switches to an American code-switched accent.

MAN (V.O.)

Well sir, I'm calling on behalf of the Phallus Clinic. And we would like to know if-

JAMIE

Phallus? Isn't that like... dicks?

MAN (V.O.)

Yes, that's correct.

Awkward silence.

JAMIE

So, you guys are the Dick Clinic then, huh?

MAN (V.O.)

Well, that's one way to put it. Our goal is to help males in any way possible as it pertains to the penis, or "dick" as you say.

JAMIE

And how's that?

MAN (V.O.)

We here believe in the teachings of our dear Dr. Freud. Especially his theory of the Phallic stage. In that, there's a focus on-

JAMIE

This sounds made up.

MAN (V.O.)

Well, uh... it isn't.

JAMIE

Yeah... I'm thinkin' it is.

MAN (V.O.)

No, this is-

JAMIE

Sounds like some kinda scam. Like those ads and pop-ups you get while watching porn.

MAN (V.O.)

Uh-

JAMIE

Silence.

Plus, you sound familiar. Almost like the piece of shit who called me a few months ago. Almost like the same guy who claimed he was from some hair loss company or some shit.

CHARLIE (V.O.)

I uh- Well, I can't lie, Jamie. I did.

JAMIE

So what? You think you can just call me about some bullshit, every once in a while, and try to scam me, right? Waste-o-fuckin space.

Pathetic.

CHARLIE (V.O.)

Sir, there's-

JAMIE

And you actually insult me by calling me thinking I'd actually go for it?

Well sir-

CHARLIE (V.O.)

JAMIE

Then you call with this fuckin' holier than thou act, like you're just a saint?

CHARLIE (V.O.)

I-

JAMIE

I bet you do this all day to everyone you can sink your little rat teeth into, right?

More silence.

CHARLIE (V.O.)

Well Jamie, when it comes to our products, we only contact those we feel are in need of them.

Jamie's face turns as he realizes what that meant.

JAMIE

Ah, suck a dick!

Jamie hangs up the phone.

DISSOLVE TO:

INT. JAMIE'S APARTMENT - BEDROOM - MORNING

The sleep of a king. The rest of a lifetime. Jamie's pillow is stained with ashy, white saliva marks. His body sprawled out like he was dropped on the bed.

INT. JAMIE'S APARTMENT - BATHROOM - LATER

Jamie stands brushing his teeth in the mirror and admiring himself. His skin even looks clearer than usual. His hair is clean-cut and slicked back. He looks as if he's sorry for other guys because... they aren't like him. They never will be.

BLACK SCREEN:

SUPER: "Three Months Later"

INT. JAMIE'S APARTMENT - BEDROOM - NIGHT

Jamie paces around his room, jittery. His eyes keep darting to the phone, then back around the room. Jamie begins a voiceover monologue as it all plays out.

JAMIE (V.O.)

This shit is like a drug by now. I can't even sleep without a hit.

Something about talking to this dick, Charlie, is like therapy... but better.

INT. JAMIE'S BEDROOM - BATHROOM - DAY

Jamie sits on his toilet lid, watching social media videos of Teddy, Peter and Leon having wild fun.

Drugged and sexual.

JAMIE (V.O.)

Those bastards hung me out to dry. They got so caught up in not having me around to be boss, they didn't even realize what I'd have to deal with as a result. Or did they? I knew right then I was gonna have to show them.

INT. JAMIE'S APARTMENT - DOORWAY - DAY

There's a soft KNOCK on the door. Jamie opens the door to reveal a girl - SARAH (19) - holding a bag of restaurant food.

JAMIE (V.O.)

Then, there was Sarah. If there was ever a nicer thing to see...

INT. JAMIE'S APARTMENT - LIVING ROOM - MOMENTS LATER

Jamie and Sarah are on his Sofa, spooning under a blanket, watching TV.

JAMIE (V.O.)

She likes it rough and she doesn't ask too many questions. What's not to like? I found her on this app, and I usually think those are shit. This time though? So far, so good.

Jamie slides his hand down Sarah's shoulder, to her

boob. She looks back to him and they lock eyes just before making out.

JAMIE (V.O.) (CONT'D)

She didn't need me to say, (mockingly)

"Oh, don't worry baby, we're a thing now, okay? You can feel secure with me. I'll always be there for you." So, I didn't. And not that I would anyway. Unless she made me feel like I should, to keep her around.

INT. JAMIE'S APARTMENT - BEDROOM - NIGHT

Back to Jamie pacing around, drooling over his phone.

JAMIE (V.O.)

That beautiful little thing. All I've gotta do is yell into it every night and BOOM... I sleep like a baby.

JAMIE

Come on... Come on.

Jamie finally picks up the phone.

INT. JAMIE'S APARTMENT - BEDROOM - LATER

Jamie and Charlie are talking on the phone, the conversation inaudible at this point.

JAMIE (V.O.)

That poor bastard, Charlie. He never seems

to get tired of it. He just keeps comin' back, taking this ass whoopin'. It's almost like he likes it. But then he really doesn't. And I can't figure out which one I'd like more.

Jamie grins as he nods his head, still inaudible.

JAMIE (V.O.) (CONT'D)

At this point, I don't think he would know what balls were if he were actually born with them. I can't help but get comfortable. All I can think is, "He's my little bit-

JAMIE

What!? You mean to tell me you never retaliate when you get disrespected?

We very slowly begin to zoom in on Jamie as he speaks for the entirety of this conversation.

CHARLIE (V.O.)

It's my job to be a professional. I don't get paid to bring my feelings to work... just my work ethic.

JAMIE

So, in other words you let people, including me, walk all over you and don't do a thing about it because it's

(MORE)

JAMIE (CONT'D)

(air quotes)

"professional"?

CHARLIE (V.O.)

Well, like I say: Your "weakness" is my "professionalism". Just because people aren't nice to you doesn't give you the right to be mean back.

JAMIE

Hey, hey, hey, I don't need a lecture on rights. I need you to just admit that you're weak.

CHARLIE (V.O.)

Sir, there's nothing wrong with being able to control your temper.

The conversation pace picks up.

JAMIE

There's nothing wrong with being able to stand up for yourself.

CHARLIE (V.O.)

That's pride.

JAMIE

Pride to stand up for yourself?

CHARLIE (V.O.)

Pride to believe you always need the last word.

JAMIE

Since when is this about the last word?

Charlie's speech changes from codeswitching to almost cold, calm, collected and direct. He could be anybody now.

CHARLIE (V.O.)

Since Man started thinkin' being the loudest in the room makes you the Alpha. It ain't the space you take up, it's what you do with it.

A dumfounded look crosses Jamie's face as he pulls the phone away from his ear to examine it. Something's not right.

JAMIE

Charlie, you good there, man? You seem a little-

CHARLIE (V.O.)

Oh, just fine, kid.

JAMIE

You just- it's like-

CHARLIE (V.O.)

You know, all this time you've been at my throat about who I am. Why don't we get to know who you are? I mean who you really are. If you even know.

Hold on-

JAMIE

CHARLIE (V.O.)

Why don't we start with your childhood?

Jamie freezes.

CHARLIE (V.O.) (CONT'D)

Well, I guess I'll lead you. Uhhh... hmm... let's start with mommy. Why didn't you tell daddy, huh? Why hate him just for the sake of it? Is it really his fault for being ignorant?

Jamie gets pale and sinks into his chair.

JAMIE

I don't- I don't wanna-

CHARLIE (V.O.)

Don't wanna what? Don't wanna talk about mommy pulling on your weeman while daddy was busy slaving away?

JAMIE

I-

CHARLIE (V.O.)

Don't even worry about it. I'll talk for you. You take advantage of girls now because it makes you feel more like a man. Like Sarah. Cute girl too. Y'all are perfect for each other, you both have daddy issues. It's so sad when guys like you can't just man up handle it yourself. You gotta suck others into it.

Jamie's eyes well up with tears.

JAMIE

(softly) How do you even-

CHARLIE (V.O.)

Don't worry, kid... I'll just show you what it feels like.

Nothing.

Charlie goes from a chuckle to a full-on laugh.

CHARLIE (V.O.) (CONT'D)

No, no, no, don't even stress it, mate. I think I'll do the hanging up this time. Give you a chance to reflect on tonight. Sleep tight, strongman.

JAMIE

I-

Charlie hangs up.

Jamie sits with tears and a look of shock plastered on his face. He drops the phone from his ear to his lap and stares into oblivion.

DISSOLVE TO:

INT. JAMIE'S APARTMENT - BEDROOM - DAY

We come back on the phone, Jamie in the background pacing again. Jamie breathing like he's just run a mile. His dark eyes and messy hair, the lack of rest plastered on his face.

INT. JAMIE'S APARTMENT - BEDROOM - NIGHT

Jamie sits on the edge of his bed with a continued gaze locked on the phone. He moves swiftly from the bed to the chair and sifts through the phone. He finds "Charlie", taps it and waits with anticipation for a response. Jamie stands up to pace around the room... again.

JAMIE

Oh, you're gonna respect me! I'm not a man, huh? I'm not a man!? We'll see... we'll see who's the man when I fuck you, huh?

The phone goes to an AUTOMATED VOICE.

AUTOMATED VOICE

The number you have dialed is not in service. Please hang up and check the number to try again.

Jamie's energy sinks into the floor just as fast as his body does. His knees slam into the floor and send a shock up through his body. His face crumples up until all he can let out is...

JAMIE

No... you can't.

He calls again. The same Automated Voice comes on.

AUTOMATED VOICE

The number-

Jamie hangs up. He checks for the number, there isn't one. He taps "Charlie" again. It goes straight to the Automated Voice.

JAMIE

THE FUCK!

Jamie throws his phone against the wall, breaking it.

DISSOLVE TO:

BLACK SCREEN

SUPER: "One Month Later"

INT. JAMIE'S APARTMENT - DINING AREA - NIGHT

Jamie squats in the corner of his dining room, not in the chairs. He's wearing a t-shirt that seems to drape over him instead of fitting around him. Looking sickly and near emaciated, he whispers to himself unintelligibly. His hair is draped over his face with an almost waxy look to it. He's wasting away.

A loud vibration comes from inside Jamie's bedroom. His head slowly lifts to see if he is hearing correctly.

INT. JAMIE'S APARTMENT - BEDROOM - MOMENTS LATER

Jamie hobbles into the room and scans the area. The phone sits on his dresser, completely broken, but somehow illuminated and vibrating. He stares for a while before picking up the phone.

Suddenly...

KNOCK KNOCK KNOCK KNOCK.

Somebody beats on the door like it may come off the hinges any second. Jamie drops his phone and backs into the wall.

INT. JAMIE'S APARTMENT - LIVING ROOM - MOMENTS LATER

Jamie slowly walks toward the door. The knocking stops just as he gets within a few feet, so does he.

He almost answers the door.

JAMIE

(hesitant)

Who-

BOOM. The door gets kicked down right on top of him, slamming his head into the floor. His vision is woozy but the best he can make out is a tall silhouette of a man with flame-like hair going in all directions, a tall black peacoat and red crocodile cowboy boots. The large, animal-covered boots crash through the wreckage as they make their way to Jamie.

Jamie comes to and tries to run. His movements are in slow- motion as he tries to escape into the bedroom.

INT. JAMIE'S APARTMENT - BEDROOM - CONTINUOUS

Jamie stumbles into the room, slams the door and falls to the floor to pick his phone up. It's broken.

JAMIE

Shit!

Behind him there's another BOOM... as the bedroom door gets smashed into splinters.

Jamie snatches his head around and in less than a second, he's off his butt... off his feet... and in the air. A black gloved hand holds him by the throat, his feet dangling. The hand releases Jamie and just as he falls, the second gloved hand punches his jaw. Jamie's lifeless body flies across the room and smashes a dent into the wall.

INT. JAMIE'S APARTMENT - BEDROOM - LATER

We now see from Jamie's POV as he starts to regain his vision. A dark cloud hovers over him. He is face up and gets turned over, face down.

BLACK OUT BACK TO SCENE

Jamie's eyes reopen as the dark cloud exits the bedroom. BLACK OUT

INT. JAMIE'S BEDROOM - LATER

Jamie wakes up in the midst of wood pieces, blood and dry wall scattered around him. His head bleeding and eye swollen. The only light is coming from another room leaking light into Jamie's bedroom. There's a chopping sound coming from the light source. Jamie drags himself to his dresser, using it to stand on his wobbly legs. He slips something on his dresser into his pocket and exits the room.

INT. DINING AREA - MOMENTS LATER

Jamie wobbles out of his room and into the dining area. The light blinds him as he stumbles into the room where he has a clear view of the DARK MAN standing in the kitchen. His wild twist out hair, well-groomed facial hair, black dress shirt, a knife holster over his shirt, black denim and the fiery, red crocodile cowboy boots - all over a tall, well-built frame. The Dark Man is chopping up food with a forearm-sized Bowie knife. His peacoat is off with an apron over his dress shirt. He notices Jamie.

DARK MAN

Well, hello there! I'd bet that was the best sleep you've gotten in a while. Well... the most, maybe not the best.

Jamie tries to speak, and he stumbles over his broken jaw. Dark Man stops chopping, stabs the knife into the cutting board and walks to Jamie.

DARK MAN (CONT'D)

Sorry about that, kid. Lemme help ya there.

Jamie tries to back away, but the Man grabs him and sits him in a chair at the dining room table.

DARK MAN (CONT'D)

There, there, Kid. Let your friend help you.

He starts massaging Jamie's jaw. Jamie looks to him in confusion.

DARK MAN (CONT'D)

It's me... Charlie.

Jamie's eyes widen and he tries to stand just as Charlie pops his jaw back into place. He yelps out and drops back into the seat.

CHARLIE

All better right?

Charlie pats Jamie on the shoulder and walks back into the kitchen. He goes back to chopping.

CHARLIE (CONT'D)

I figured I'd fix you a nice meal so we

could get down to business while you're on a full stomach.

Jamie stands and Charlie snaps his head over to him with a look as if to say "Sit!". Jamie plops down in the seat immediately, holding his face.

CHARLIE (CONT'D)

Right.

Charlie grabs a bowl and fills it with the chopped chicken, potatoes and vegetables. He then fills it with a liquid that was sitting in a pot on the stovetop. Charlie puts his knife in his holster and makes his way from the kitchen to the dining room with the bowl and sits it in front of Jamie.

CHARLIE (CONT'D)

Bon Appétit.

Jamie stares at the bowl in confusion.

CHARLIE (CONT'D)

Ah! I forgot the spoon, huh? Un momento.

Charlie walks back into the kitchen and grabs a spoon, comes back to Jamie and slides it in the bowl.

CHARLIE (CONT'D)

Well, what do we say?

He puts two fingers to his ear to listen in.

JAMIE

Thanks.

CHARLIE

No problem, kid.

Charlie slaps Jamie's shoulder and inches closer as he keeps talking to Jamie.

CHARLIE (CONT'D)

This problem you have with your self-image... I'm gonna straighten that out for you. That's all I plan to do here. Nurse a little birdie back to health. Put the MAN back in this little lady here.

He rubs Jamie's shoulder.

CHARLIE (CONT'D)

EAT.

Jamie slowly picks up the spoon, dips it in the bowl and comes back up with a full spoon. He stares at it for a second and then looks to Charlie, who is grinning with anticipation.

CHARLIE (CONT'D)

Go on there, slurp it on in.

He grabs Jamie's hand and pushes the spoon to his mouth. Jamie finally slurps it in and swallows.

CHARLIE (CONT'D)

Good.

(back to rubbing shoulders) I want you not to stress here because we're gonna get through

this together, alright? Don't even stress it baby boy, you'll be good as new in no time.

While rubbing Jamie's shoulder, Charlie moves so close that his crotch is now on Jamie's shoulder. Jamie almost chokes as he gulps the food down in surprise.

CHARLIE (CONT'D)

What's wrong, Jamie? Is it too bland? Too seasoned? Maybe just not your speed.

Jamie tries to shuffle away from Charlie. Suddenly, a KNOCK on the door. Both males turn and look at the door. Charlie smiles.

CHARLIE (CONT'D)

Well, if I had to guess... I'd say that's our darling Sarah. Maybe she'll want some of my special soup. And this chicken stuff too, I guess.

Charlie chuckles as Jamie turns his head to look at Charlie's crotch, then the bowl.

JAMIE

Mother-

Jamie smacks the bowl against the wall breaking it.

He jumps out of his seat and backs away from Charlie. Charlie laughs with his hands up as he walks closer to Jamie, forcing him to back away closer to the wall.

CHARLIE

Don't stress it, kid. I'll just invite her in. You go on and sit back down.

Charlie walks away, Jamie doesn't sit so he stops to flash him another serious look. Jamie sits back down. Charlie walks to the door and unlocks it. Before fading into the shadow behind it. The door opens from the inside on its own, and Sarah eases in.

SARAH

Jamie?

Sarah walks further in and looks to Jamie, who is sitting at the table, shaking.

SARAH (CONT'D)

Are you okay, Ja-

Charlie emerges behind her.

CHARLIE

Well hello, cutie.

Sarah screams and turns to him.

CHARLIE (CONT'D)

I already thought you were good looking, but now... to see you with my own eyes...

He walks toward her, and she backs away to Jamie.

SARAH

Jamie, who is this?

CHARLIE

(to Jamie) Don't get up.

Jamie doesn't.

SARAH

Jamie?

Just as she turns to Jamie, Charlie grabs her by the hair and drags her to the side of the table opposite Jamie. Kicking and screaming, Sarah ends up on her knees. Jamie stands and stretches his arms out.

JAMIE

Please. Please don't do anything to her.

CHARLIE

Come on man you didn't even really care about her. She was just the help. Plus, I told you not to stand up.

Charlie snatches her toward him. Jamie closes his lids hard enough to crush his eyeballs. There's a scream, silenced by a crunching sound, followed by a thud. There's another thud on the table in front of

Jamie. He opens his watery eyes, no words.

CHARLIE (CONT'D)

I'll give you a head start. Let's say... ten seconds.

Jamie back against the wall frozen, no response.

CHARLIE (CONT'D)

TEN! NINE!

Charlie walks toward Jamie, who pulls a pocketknife from his jeans.

CHARLIE (CONT'D)

(laughing)

Really!? What type of faggot shit is that?

Charlie pulls out his giant Bowie knife, dwarfing Jamie's little blade.

CHARLIE (CONT'D)

EIGHT!

Jamie runs past Charlie and out of the apartment. Charlie stands for a moment, then stops counting aloud. He looks to the table, with Sarah's head and chuckles.

EXT. JAMIE'S APARTMENT - NIGHT

Jamie sprints out of his apartment and runs into his angry Neighbor from upstairs. A man with more hair than skin.

NEIGHBOR

There you are! I was just coming down here to you. I would appreciate it if you would-

Charlie's giant blade smashes through the Neighbor's back and out his stomach.

JAMIE

Shit!

Jamie runs out into the complex. Charlie yanks his blade out of the dying Neighbor's back and stares him down. His eyes widen as if to say, "Die sooner!" and the life leaves the man's eyes. Charlie cleans the blade off on his peacoat and marches on toward Jamie.

CHARLIE

(singing) Jamie, my darling!

Jamie looks back to see Charlie making his way over the hill, just walking. He turns and sprints down to the front of the community.

EXT. COMMUNITY OFFICE - MOMENTS LATER

We see Jamie flying around the corner of a wooded area of the community. He makes his way to the office. Jamie comes right to the office and gets blindsided by Charlie, who pushes Jamie into the office window. Charlie follows him in laughing.

EXT. POOL AREA - MOMENTS LATER

In the pool area behind the office, there's rustling from inside the office, which we don't see. Jamie gets thrown out of the second-story window and into the poolside seats. His shirt tattered and barely hanging on. His body covered in cuts from the glass.

Charlie puts his knife in his coat as he comes down through the building stairwell. He finds Jamie attempting to pull himself out of the broken chairs.

CHARLIE

Why even run at this point?

Jamie attempts to crawl away as Charlie snatches him back into his crotch by the hair. Jamie writhes in pain as he's lifted higher and has to hold on to Charlie for dear life.

CHARLIE (CONT'D)

Awwww. Tsk, tsk, tsk. Now, you'll just have to die like a bitch.

Jamie looks up to Charlie and spits blood in his face. Charlie explodes in laughter as Jamie yanks out his knife and plunges it into his chest. Charlie looks down at the knife unfazed.

CHARLIE (CONT'D)

Really?

Charlie uses his free hand to punch Jamie in the ribs so hard he flies across the pool area. Charlie pulls the knife from his chest and throws it into the water. Jamie now wheezing as he tries to hold his body together while face down on the ground. Charlie walks and stands directly over Jamie with his hands on his hips. His head held high.

CHARLIE (CONT'D)

For a weak one, you really do have a lot of fight in ya. I'm almost impressed! Most people would've quit back at the broken jaw, but you-

Jamie quickly turns and rams Charlie's Bowie knife into his heart. Charlie looks down to his chest, this time in shock, the huge blade handle pointed out. Charlie chuckles and spits up blood.

CHARLIE (CONT'D)

Hm… what a crafty little shit. When'd you get that?

JAMIE

Who's the bitch now?

CHARLIE

(laughing)

Oh, it's still you.

Charlie stumbles toward the pool and falls in it. His blood slowly spreading across the water. Jamie falls back, lying on the ground and looking up to the stars. Blood still leaking from his body.

EXT. COMMUNITY OFFICE - LATER

Jamie wobbles away from the pool entrance, to the front of the office and sits on the curb. He holds his body and examines his wounds. After a while, there's a vibration in his pocket. He slides a phone out, this one isn't his. At least not the broken one. Jamie reads the Caller ID.

HOLD ON JAMIE'S FACE. We can't see who's calling, but he can. The ID he sees on the phone makes him take a few shuttered breathes and sharply turn his head toward the pool area.

THE END

MAULDIN COUNTY

MAULDIN COUNTY

written by

Caleze

What is "FOREVER"?

SUN MOON AND THREE LESS STARS

EXT. DESERT HIGHWAY - NIGHT, 1969

Somewhere out West, a black, Dodge Charger speeds down an empty highway. The windows are too darkly tinted to see inside, and the car is going too fast to catch a glimpse regardless. Thunder can be heard as rain clouds form across the sky. The Charger whips us into a view of a "Welcome to Mauldin County" sign.

EXT. THE SUNNY MOTEL - LATER

Outside of a blue and white-themed motel, a couple steps out of a green VW Bus. The man - RILEY - and the woman - SUE - carelessly stand in the pouring rain. Riley, an average sized guy wearing flip flops, a Rolling Stones t-shirt, shorts and a caveman style beard and hair combo. Sue, a blonde-haired, blue-eyed girl is wearing large, round glasses, a cutoff tank top, blue jean shorts and flip flops as well.

RILEY

(stretching)

It's room C1 right?

SUE

(arms crossed)

Uhhh... sure.

RILEY

We don't know?

SUE

We?

RILEY

Yeah babe... “we”.

SUE

Well, I guess *we* better ask *your* friend.

Sue pats Riley on the shoulder condescendingly.

RILEY

My friend, huh? Since when is any hitchhiker just MY friend?

SUE

Since you didn't force him to respect our van.

RILEY

(unsure)

Well... he didn't disrespect it.

SUE

Really?

Sue's arms recross and she gives Riley a piercing stare.

RILEY

I'll just go get him.

Riley walks to the other side of the van and opens

the door to reveal - JOE - a stoner with a loud, button-down, tie-dye shirt, baggy brown pants, Converse and a bandana wrapped around his long, blonde hair. Riley shoves Joe, waking him up abruptly.

JOE

(startled)

Whoa, buddy! All good?

RILEY

We're here.

JOE

Oh, far out, man.

He sits up and collects himself, patting his shirt and pants pockets.

JOE (CONT'D)

They have cigarettes in there?

RILEY

Nobody smokes... cigarettes.

JOE

Who- Who doesn't smoke cigarettes?

RILEY

Come on man let's go. We're already late.

Joe slides out of the car and Riley walks towards Sue who looks fed up, after being in the rain this long.

JOE

Hey, bud, you mind if I borrow the van to get some cigs from the store? I'm fallin' apart here.

RILEY

(looks to Sue first)

I can't give you the keys, but if you need wheels there's a board in the back.

Joe peers through the window to see the skateboard in the backseat.

JOE

Right on! I'll be back momentarily.

He jumps in the van and shimmy to the back. Sue and Riley make their way to the Clerk's Office.

INT. CLERK'S OFFICE - MOMENTS LATER

Sue and Riley step into the office dripping water everywhere, but the CLERK doesn't seem to mind. He seems more worried about his crossword puzzle to notice.

RILEY

Hey, friend. There's a group of about

three to four people who got a room.

The Clerk never looks up from his book.

CLERK

On this weekend? That's almost every room.

SUE

The name on it should be Mary Callahan. Maybe room C1?

The Clerk's eyes peer over his glasses to get a good look at the couple.

CLERK

B1. And make sure you remind them not to let that little mutt break anything.

SUE

Of course! Thanks.

(to Riley)

Let's go.

The couple leave the office as the Clerk tracks them with his eyes before resuming his puzzle.

EXT. IN-TOWN MAULDIN - NIGHT

Joe rides the skateboard, weaving from sidewalk to street as he slides through town. The black Charger flies by Joe almost causing him to wobble.

JOE

Shit!

He manages to stay on the board as he comes to a stop. The car disappears around the corner a block away.

JOE (CONT'D)

What a dick.

He puts the board back in the street and continues skating down the street. After a few seconds, the Charger pulls back up behind Joe and slowly stalks him. Joe, thinking it's a car just passing by skates back onto the sidewalk. The car continues slowly enough to track his speed. When Joe notices, he cuts his eyes at the car repeatedly before taking off. His leg is moving so fast he's practically running on one foot.

The car speeds up to match him, the engine roaring with aggression. Just as he reaches the crosswalk, the car moves right in front of him and slams on breaks, sending Joe over the hood of the car and into the street.

JOE (CONT'D)

(laying on the ground)

The hell, man!?

Holding his arm, he lifts his head to look at the car, which is still sitting in the same spot. The person inside - unseen

- just watching him.

JOE (CONT'D)

What's your problem?

The Charger does a burnout and disappears down the street. Joe shuffles to his feet rubbing his arm. He looks to the skateboard which is still pretty intact.

INT. ROOM B1 - LATER

Two girls and a guy are in the hotel room setting up party items like beer, weed and snacks. The two girls - MARY and LILY - look almost identical (but not related) with their brunette hair, bikini tops, knitted shorts and sandals. The guy - WILL - has on a vest over his sleeveless, denim shirt, jeans and boots.

MARY

(to Lily)

You think we have enough?

LILY

Can you ever have enough?

MARY

Well, I mean for Sue. Last time she seemed kinda bummed.

LILY

I mean, that's just Sue. I love Sue, but if this gesture and these good things...

(playing with some blunts)

don't mellow her out, then I don't know what will.

MARY

Yeah, I guess.

Will walks out of the bathroom (closing the door) and puts his arms around them.

WILL

(smiling)

Come on ladies, it'll be a gas.

There's a knock at the door.

WILL (CONT'D)

I got it.

Will strolls to the door and snatches it open with his arms up. Sue and Riley are standing on the other side with Riley in the same pose as Will.

RILEY

What's up, Doc!?

WILL

Get in here buddy!

The boys jump into each other's arms and hug it out while laughing and slinging water everywhere. Sue with her arms crossed and a fake smile, steps into the room as Mary and Lily come to greet her.

MARY

Hey, darling. How are you?

LILY

Hey.

SUE

Hey, how are you guys?

MARY AND LILY

Great, great.

They give each other an awkward pat-hug.

LILY (CONT'D)

Well, come on in. We've got some stuff here for you.

The girls walk further into the room. The boys stay at the door and continue talking indistinctly.

MARY

(to Sue)

Oh, we've got Max here too.

Mary opens the bathroom door and out comes a German Shepherd. Sue drops to her knees and pets the frantically happy dog with a smile reading the only true emotion she's shown since she got here.

SUE

(puppy voice)

Hey, buddy! It's been a long time, huh? Yes it-

There's another knock at the door. Everybody in the room stops talking and looks to the door, then back to each other. Riley walks to the door.

RILEY

Oh yeah, we had a guy who came with us his name is-

He opens the door to reveal a couple - ISLA and FISH - standing with friendly smiles. The couple is brown-skinned and physically fit - Fish with amazing abs and Isla with noticeable dancer legs-, both with jet black, long hair. Isla is wearing a tribal dress, an anklet, bracelets and no shoes. Fish is in a cowboy hat, half undone button-down, a teeth necklace, black bellbottoms and moccasins. Mary speaks from the back.

FISH

Oh, hey there, folks. We were just in town and a new friend of ours, and I'm guessin' a friend of yours, told us about a good ole get together. For a little lady named Sue, nonetheless.

Sue stands and turns around to face the door.

FISH (CONT'D)

(to Sue)

I'm guessin' that makes you, Sue?

ISLA

(to everyone)

I'm Isla and this is Fish. If we're intruding-

MARY

No, no, no. Come on in.

Fish tips his hat to Mary.

ISLA

Thanks.

Isla and Fish walk into the room, Riley shuts the door behind them.

MARY

So, you say a friend of ours?

FISH

Uh, yeah. I don't remember the guy's name, but he was about yay high.

Fish, being tall, hovers his hand at about average height.

ISLA

And he wore these glasses that hung around his neck.

LILY

Richard?

ISLA

Yeah, him

FISH

Really funny guy. He said we wouldn't be imposing if we dropped by and brought a peace pipe.

Fish pulls a sack out of his pocket and tosses it to Will. Will holds it with a giddy look and smells.

WILL

Any friend of peace is a friend of ours.

Will smiles and walks to the back where the other party supplies are set up.

MARY

(with a smile)

Of course. No problem at all.

MARY (CONT'D)

Make yourself at home... or I guess, however much you could do that here.

The room settles and everyone seems to operate like normal. Everyone but Sue, who squats back down to pet the dog. Never taking her eyes off of Isla and Fish. Fish sits down in a chair and Isla sits on his lap. Lily walks over to the new couple and lies across the bed beside them.

LILY

So, where you guys from?

FISH

Well, here and there.

ISLA

We're drifters so it kinda varies night to night.

LILY

Ah that's really cool! I've been trying to talk Richard into it, but he's not fully sold on it.

FISH

And Richard is your...

LILY

Boyfriend. Yeah.

FISH

Well, if it ain't just another cute couple.

ISLA

We meet a lot out here when we travel and it's still one of our favorite things to see.

Lily blushes.

LILY

Well, thanks. I hope he's back soon.

FISH

Aw he should be back anytime now. The run didn't seem like it would take too long.

Mary and Sue stand in a corner of the room, talking. Sue's eyes locked on Isla and Fish.

SUE

Is it just me or do they seem kinda weird?

Weird how?

MARY

SUE

I don't know. I- they just make me feel uneasy.

MARY

Well, they are super handsy, but I would be too if Will looked anything like him.

SUE

Well-

MARY

Shit! I forgot the radio.

Mary sighs and walks to the center of the room.

MARY (CONT'D)

Hey everybody, I forgot to bring the radio and there isn't one here, so-

FISH

I have music.

MARY

You do?

FISH

Yup. Not the traditional music you're thinking of by way of radio, but I have something for us.

Isla smiles and rubs his chest.

RILEY

Hey, any music works, friend.

FISH

Great!

Fish taps Isla's butt to let him up and she jumps from his lap. Just as he turns to walk out, Isla pulls him back to French kiss. After licking his lips and winking to Isla, he walks to the door and opens it.

FISH (CONT'D)

I'll be back momentarily.

Fish leaves the room.

EXT. SUNNY MOTEL - CONTINUOUS

We follow Fish out to the hallway, then to the parking lot. A little kid is standing in the window of a room as Fish approaches the lot. Fish looks back and waves at the kid, who waves back to him. Fish turns back and heads into the lot.

EXT. SUNNY MOTEL - LATER

Joe rolls into the lot on the skateboard, smoking a cigarette as he approaches the door to the Clerk's Office.

INT. CLERK'S OFFICE - CONTINUOUS

Joe walks into the office, his board now in the opposite hand of his cigarette. He walks to the desk and the Clerk doesn't look up.

CLERK

Hey-

JOE

ROOM B1!

Joe looks shocked and eases back.

JOE

Okay then, gramps. Got it.

CLERK

(looks to Joe)

And tell 'em not to let that dumb mutt mess anything up!

Joe gives the Clerk an "okay" with the cigarette hand and walks out. The Clerk tries to resume his puzzle and instead slams the book down and walks into the back of the office.

EXT. SUNNY MOTEL - MOMENTS LATER

Joe stands under a staircase by the parking lot and lights another cigarette. As he takes a puff, he notices a black car out in the distance. It's the black Charger. Suddenly, Fish walks out from the hallway, waves at a window and continues on to the Charger.

After shuffling around in his trunk, Fish pulls a big black case and makes his way back through the hallway (all from Joe's perspective). Joe drops his cigarette and his face scrunches up. He walks towards him with determination in every step.

EXT. ROOM B1 - MOMENTS LATER

Joe approaches the door to room B1. Music can be heard from the inside. He knocks then puts his ear to the door. The door flies open, bringing Joe stumbling in. Lily's at the door and everyone else is gathered around Fish playing guitar. Everything stops when Joe enters.

LILY

Oh, I thought you were Richard. Hello, stranger. You in the right place?

JOE

Sorry, I-

Riley jumps up and waves Joe in.

RILEY

Oh yeah, that's Joe. The guy I was telling you about. He came with us.

LILY

The more, the merrier.

As Joe walks in, he starts pushing the water from his hair to the ground.

JOE

Thanks a bunch.

Mary leans into Fish while she's sitting beside him.

MARY

So, are y'all Native or something?

FISH

Well, actually-

Joe rushes in towards Fish with his finger pointed.

JOE

You're the bastard that tried to run me over earlier!

Isla stands up immediately and shoves her hand into Joe's chest, stopping him in his tracks. The whole room stands quietly. Fish puts his guitar down and stands up.

FISH

(hands up, smiling)

Peace, brother. I don't really know what you're talkin' about, but I'm sure we could figure this out.

JOE

You stalked me and then tried to run me over with your stupid car!

FISH

(looks to the skateboard on the floor)

Ah! You were the skateboard feller huh?

JOE

Yeah!

FISH

Well, apologies, brother. I must not have noticed you. One second you were on the sidewalk and the next, I couldn't even see you. We felt the bump but didn't even recognize it was a person.

(laughing)

Lotta stray dogs around these parts.

JOE

You mother-

Fish puts his hand on Joe's shoulder and pulls the blunt from Isla's hand and motioning her back.

FISH

Why don't you let me make it up to you?

Joe looks at the blunt and he’s stuck. There’s a long pause before the aggression seems to release.

JOE

Well, I guess we ought to let bygones be bygones.

Joe takes the blunt and everyone except Isla and Fish clap.

FISH

Alright then! Let's get back to it.

MARY

Finally!

Fish goes back to his spot on the bed with his guitar. Isla and Fish's eyes meet, and they smile. He plucks a few strings and goes into a song.

CUT TO BLACK.

EXT. SUNNY MOTEL - NIGHT

An old, pickup truck pulls into the parking lot of the motel. A YOUNG MAN wearing a baseball cap, a t-shirt, jeans and cowboy boots exits the truck. He pulls a few bags from the passenger seat, shuts the door and we follow him down the hallway to the rooms.

EXT. ROOM B1 - CONTINUOUS

He reaches the door of Room B1 and knocks. The door creaks open to reveal Mary, Will, Riley, Sue and Joe all laying across the floor and some on the walls. Their bodies all dismembered and rearranged. The ones with eyes hold fear in them, the others missing heads. The young man stumbles backward and drops his bag. Max, the dog, runs out of the room yelping, seemingly unharmed. We close in on the contents that slide out from the bag. Two bracelets - one reads "Lily" and the other reads "Richard".

EXT. DESERT HIGHWAY - MOMENTS LATER

Fish in the driver seat and Isla in the passenger, the two ride down the highway laughing hysterically. They alternate between kissing and laughing until we get a shot outside the car, riding down the long stretch.

CUT TO BLACK.

BLACK SCREEN

SUPER: "Atlanta, Georgia 2016"

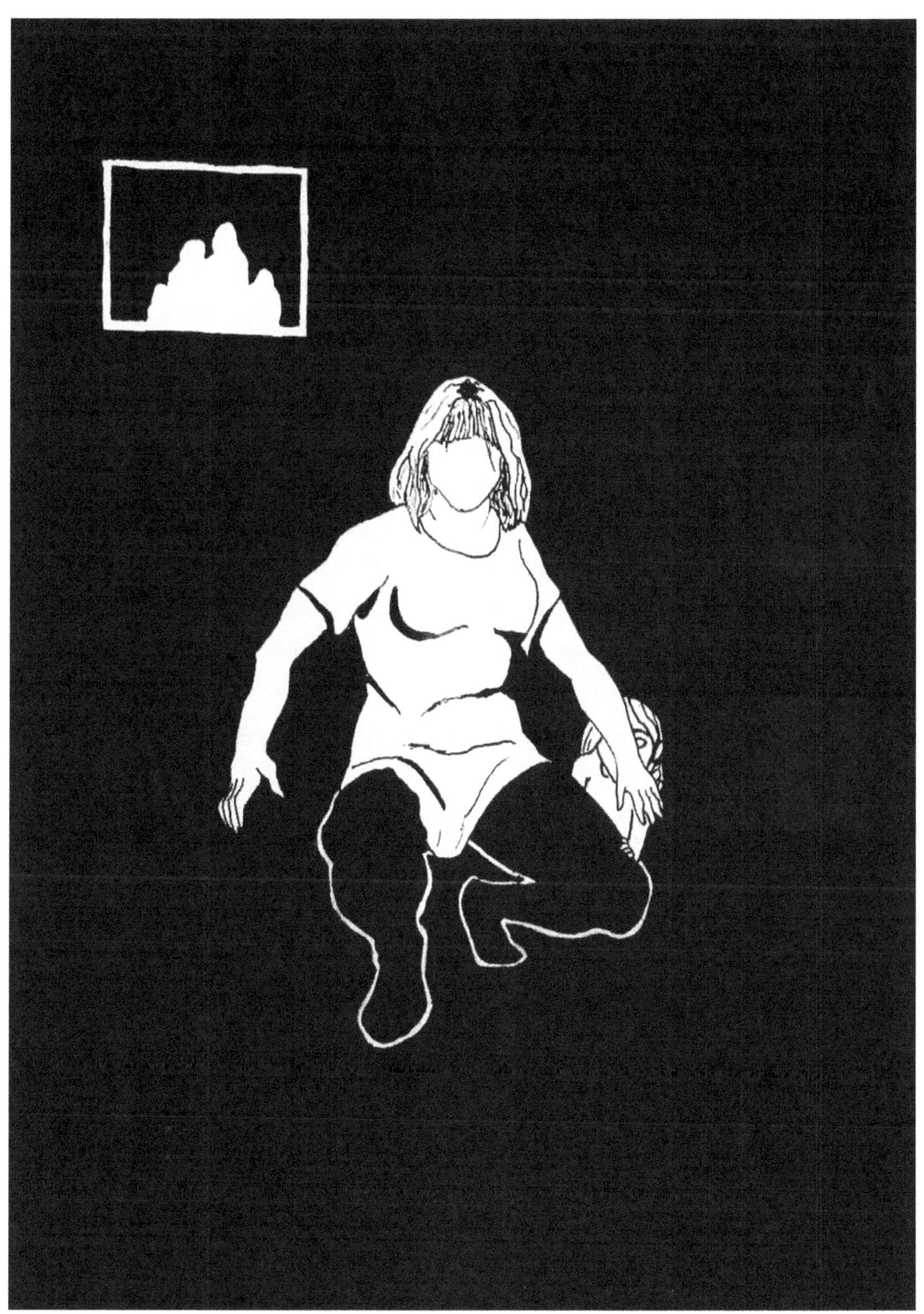

EXT. HIGHWAY I-285 - DAY

A black Dodge Challenger stutters through traffic on the Atlanta highway.

It's rush hour and cars aren't exactly bumper to bumper yet, but there are enough cars that they can barely go half of the speed limit.

INT. ISLA & FISH'S CHALLENGER - MOMENTS LATER

As usual, Fish is driving and Isla is in the passenger seat, with the addition of being on her phone. They look exactly the same as they did in the 60's (no aging), and their style is similar with the exception of a modern upgrade. Isla now has short, blonde hair. Fish's non-driving leg is jumping and he's tapping his fingers on the steering wheel to the music only he hears. He looks back and forth from Isla on her phone and the road.

FISH

(smiling)

That's the one thing I can't get used to about Atlanta: so much traffic.

He looks to Isla for a response... nothing.

FISH (CONT'D)

Ya know?

Isla finally looks to him.

ISLA

Know what?

FISH

(face drops)

Nothing.

Isla looks back to her phone.

ISLA

You could always just say it, but you never do.

FISH

Yeah, well you could always just listen to me the first time instead of always being on that stupid phone.

ISLA

When you have something interesting to say and not just fluffy charm, then maybe I'll put the phone down.

Fish's leg is jumping faster now as he exhales deeply and pops his neck. His eyes never leave the road. The two sit in complete silence for a while until Fish turns on the radio. Isla turns the volume down and resumes scrolling on her phone.

EXT. HARDWARE STORE LOT - NIGHT

The Challenger speeds into a hardware store parking lot and whips into a spot.

INT. ISLA & FISH'S CHALLENGER - CONTINUOUS

Fish turns the car off and looks to Isla, still on her phone.

FISH

You want something?

ISLA

Nope.

Fish takes the key out of the ignition and exits the car.

EXT. HARDWARE STORE LOT - CONTINUOUS

As Fish walks away a MAN stops him and points at his car.

MAN

That's yo' car, man?

FISH

(smirking) Yessir.

MAN

That's dope man, I been wantin' me one of those.

FISH

Yeah, it's the only American muscle that looks kinda old school.

MAN

Aye man that's for sure. You know-

INT. ISLA & FISH'S CHALLENGER - CONTINUOUS

Isla looks behind her to examine the conversation between the Man and Fish. She smacks her teeth, sinks further into the seat and resumes scrolling on her phone. We finally get a view of what she's looking at - babies. Her social media feed is flooded with babies and families, and the occasional dog or house post. A tear forms in her eye. She's so enamored with the pictures and videos that she jumps when Fish opens the door and hops in.

FISH

(noticing her face)

You good?

ISLA

(wiping her eyes as she looks away)

Yeah.

FISH

(with a sigh)

You know, it only works if you actually talk to me when there's an issue. Not just throwin' your shade and leaving it alone.

Isla with her eyes dry, looks back to Fish.

ISLA

How'd you get back so fast.

FISH

Fast? I was in there ten minutes.

Fish throws a store bag in Isla's lap. She opens it to find ropes and duct tape. Fish turns the car on and backs out of the space, leaving her to examine these items with a tired look.

EXT. MANSION - NIGHT

Around 1 A.M., a large party of people dressed in dapper attire exit a sizable Atlanta mansion. The party makes their way to their expensive, luxury cars in the roundabout of the house. They wave their goodbyes to the couple of the house, standing in the doorway, seeing them off. The couple - MR. & MRS. HARRIS -

INT. MANSION KITCHEN - LATER

Mr. Harris walks into the kitchen where GLORIA the maid is cleaning the remainder of the dishes from the party.

GLORIA

Hola, Mr. Harris. I will be out of your kitchen soon.

MR. HARRIS

No rush, Gloria. I really appreciate it.

Mr. Harris grabs a drink from the refrigerator and walks back to the kitchen doorway.

MR. HARRIS (CONT'D)

Please don't stay up too late. You can always leave a few things until the morning since you'll be here anyway.

GLORIA

(with a laugh)

No, senor. I will finish it tonight. Sweet dreams.

MR. HARRIS

Okay then, goodnight.

Mr. Harris exits, and Gloria continues. After a few seconds, the lights start flickering. Gloria looks around and after seeing nothing, she returns to work. As she looks back to the dishes, Fish appears behind Gloria. He's breathing on her so heavily that she turns and screams, throwing herself against the counter, then to the ground. Fish steps over her and extends his hand. She hesitates for a while before taking it and getting up. Fish nods his head toward the door as if to say "Get outta here", and she does just that. Gloria runs to another room of the house to disappear for good.

A door upstairs opens and footsteps creak toward the staircase. Fish fades into the shadows. Mrs. Harris is revealed at the stairs, making her way down.

MRS. HARRIS

Gloria, are you okay, hun'?

Just as she reaches the bottom, Fish comes out and rips her throat out. Mrs. Harris drops to the floor and gurgles blood as Fish steps over her and moves upstairs.

INT. HARRIS' BEDROOM - MOMENTS LATER

Mr. Harris is lying on his king-size bed, his back to the door, reading a book. The door slightly creaks open, and a silhouette slides through with no sound.

MR. HARRIS

(eyes still on his book)

Honey, what seemed to be the problem?

No response.

MR. HARRIS (CONT'D)

Honey?

Mr. Harris turns on his back to look at "his wife". Isla stands over him and rams her fist through Mr. Harris' chest, leaving him wheezing in an attempt to scream out. His shocked look fades as Isla's aggression increases. Isla grunts her way out of the bedroom and into the hallway.

INT. CHILD'S BEDROOM - MOMENTS LATER

We are in female child's room, pink-colored and fluffy with a child's decorative imagination. That child - OLIVIA (6) - is sleeping in her equally decorative bed. Her door creaks open. A silhouette crawls through with no sound. Her precious face is overshadowed by Isla who crawls over her back and slowly peels the cover back. Isla inhales rigidly and opens her mouth wide. Her canines grow abnormally long and lunges toward Olivia. Just as she's close enough to bite the child, Isla pauses, and her canines retract. Isla pulls back and moves to get a better look at the child's face. Olivia's innocence captivates Isla as she softly rubs the princess' face with her bloody hand. Isla stands and shakes the child.

ISLA

Baby, you've gotta get up!

Olivia's eyes snap open and she screams as she looks at Isla.

ISLA (CONT'D)

No, no, no. It's okay, I'm here to help you. Your mommy and daddy had an accident and I need to get you out of here.

OLIVIA

(calming down)

What do you mean?

ISLA

Do you have a neighbor near here that you can go to?

OLIVIA

Umm... yes.

ISLA

(motherlike while holding Olivia's hands)

Okay, and who's that?

OLIVIA

Mrs. Handler.

ISLA

Okay, great. So, we need to get your robe on, and I need you to run there as fast as you can no matter what, okay?

OLIVIA

Okay...

Isla stands Olivia up and puts her robe on.

OLIVIA (CONT'D)

Where's my mommy and daddy?

Isla stops to kneel down to Olivia's level.

ISLA

Well, like I said darling, they were in

an accident and you can't see them yet. But you're gonna be just fine okay, darling?

OLIVIA

(wiping hcr eyes)

Okay.

ISLA

Great, now let's go.

Isla stands and holds Olivia's hand as she leads her out of the room.

INT. FOYER - CONTINUOUS

Isla and Olivia rush down the staircase and just as they reach the door, Fish emerges from a room upstairs with a young girl - EMMA (18) - hogtied and gagged with duct tape. Fish's eyes bloodshot and his fangs out.

FISH

Isla, the hell are you doing?

Olivia screams as she gets a look at her unconscious sister. Isla snatches the front door open and pulls Olivia outside.

ISLA

Run kid, run!

Olivia runs out of her driveway screaming and crying. Isla turns back to Fish and slams the door behind her.

Fish reaches the bottom of the stairs and drops Emma on her stomach.

FISH

Now, why exactly would you do that?

ISLA

We've got more than enough to eat. We don't need a child.

FISH

And what gave you the right to make that decision?

ISLA

Pfft, who are you? God?

FISH

No, just the person who used to have a relationship. Who intended on holding that together. I'm the guy who can't seem to get my wife-

ISLA

DON'T CALL ME THAT!

Isla's fangs grow back, and her bloodshot eyes lock onto Fish's. Fish scoffs, picks Emma up and walks her to Isla.

FISH

Since you have such a soft spot for little bitches, take this one.

Fish shoves Emma into Isla's arms and walks away.

FISH (CONT'D)

I'll grab the other two.

Fish walks back upstairs. Isla is left holding Emma and calming herself as her appearance returns to normal.

INT. AIRBNB - NIGHT

A few hours after leaving the Harris residence, Isla and Fish arrive at their Airbnb, Fish snatching the door open and checks his phone to compare what he sees with what was advertised. Isla unenthusiastically eases in behind him, rolling a giant suitcase. Fish does a walkthrough of the house and lands in the master bedroom.

INT. AIRBNB BEDROOM - CONTINUOUS

Paintings, a bed, a 60-inch flatscreen, updated bathroom, thc works.

FISH

(not to Isla)

Good enough.

Fish walks back out of the room. Isla kicks her shoes off, rolls the suitcase beside the bed and hops on it. After a little while staring at the paintings on the wall, Isla exhales deeply and shifts over to open the suitcase. Emma falls out and smacks her face on the floor, groaning.

ISLA

(lifting Emma)

Here we go.

Isla puts Emma on the bed beside her, cuts her legs loose and sits the girl upright.

ISLA (CONT'D)

Comfortable?

Emma moans through the duct tape and more tears roll out. Isla grabs the remote, turns the tv on and dries Emma's eyes.

ISLA (CONT'D)

You wanna watch the news or Animal Planet? Well...

(chuckling)

maybe not the news because you might see your parents on there.

Emma cries harder.

ISLA (CONT'D)

(gets serious)

I'm sorry. That was mean. Maybe we just watch a little.

INSERT - TV SCREEN

A female ANCHOR for a 24-hour news circuit reports with images and B-roll beside her.

ANCHOR

Today, a man was caught with a dog sex ring in his basement. Will Tavern was busted just yesterday by police, who were anonymously tipped off.

ANCHOR (CONT'D)

Neighbors, out-of-towners and even foreigners would travel to Tavern's home to have sex with dogs ranging from puppies to old and dying.

BACK TO SCENE

Isla shakes her head and looks to Emma.

ISLA

People are sick, huh?

Emma looks to her in confusion. INSERT - TV SCREEN

The Anchor transitions.

ANCHOR

In a bit of a flashback of sorts, we remember the anniversary of the Sunny Motel Murders of 1969. Five were murdered in a motel room after a night of partying. The only surviving members were Richard Banks and his dog Max. At the time, they were seen as a potential Manson Murder copycat. Now, detective Alan Murphy isn't so sure-

BACK TO SCENE

Isla sighs and turns to Emma.

ISLA

That was us a long time ago. We killed a bunch of stoners and made it look like a fan of old Charlie did it.

(sad laugh)

We always thought if people knew what we were, we'd end up like some kinda Area 51 or MK Ultra shit.

(she starts crying)

We pick a stupid ass day out of the year and drain privileged people.

It was fun when we were younger, but now-

(sniffling and rubbing her eyes)

We've been around so long that-

Fish walks in holding Mr. And Mrs. Harris wrapped in plastic. Emma screams through the duct tape and tries to get up.

FISH

First of all, why did you untie her legs? Second, why in the world would you tell her about us?

Isla sits Emma back and stands up.

ISLA

Oh, shut up!

FISH

See? This is why people end up tortured before we - I mean I... kill them. We could do this so easy, but you make it harder when you keep these little pets and whine on and on about-

Isla gets in his face.

ISLA

I'm tired of this shit! All of it! You want me to just be okay still but-

Fish walks away from her and into the bathroom.

ISLA (CONT'D)

Oh, so you're just gonna ignore me now?

Fish comes back out of the bathroom without the bodies and walks past Isla and out of the door.

ISLA (CONT'D)

(to Emma)

I just can't stand him anymore. He just doesn't even respect me now and then he wants me to be nice about it.

Emma shakes on the bed groaning and shrugging. Fish walks back in with a duffle bag and walks into the bathroom. Isla stands with her arms crossed, tracking Fish's movements with her eyes. Fish comes out of the bathroom empty handed and leaves the room.

EXT. AIRBNB - MOMENTS LATER

Fish hops in the car and speeds off. Isla stands in the window watching, before angrily shutting the blinds.

EXT. GAS STATION - MORNING

It's just before dawn, right as the clouds have taken on that orange hue. Fish flies into a gas station parking lot and exits the car. He stops to look at the sky, then his watch.

FISH

Dang, I'm runnin' outta time.

Fish jogs into the gas station.

INT. GAS STATION - CONTINUOUS

There's nobody but the CLERK in the station, and as he notices Fish, he stops sweeping and returns to the counter.

CLERK

Welcome in.

FISH

How's it goin', partner.

CLERK

Can't complain.

Fish walks around looking through each aisle.

CLERK (CONT'D)

Looking for something specific?

FISH

Yeah, rubbing alcohol?

CLERK

(motioning to an aisle) Aisle seven there.

FISH

Thanks.

Fish walks over to the aisle and grabs every bottle of alcohol he sees. He walks to the counter and lays it all out for the Clerk.

CLERK

Wow, you think you got enough?

FISH

Never can be too safe right?

CLERK

I guess not.

Before the Clerk starts ringing Fish up, an older, white WOMAN walks in and stands behind Fish, looking him up and down. Fish turns his head to her and nods with a smile. The Woman gives him a look of disgust, clutches her purse and turns her head. Fish is taken aback, but just turns back to the Clerk.

WOMAN

You think you could hurry this along? I have a class to be at.

Both men ignore her.

WOMAN (CONT'D)

Hello!? I just need cigarettes and you see me walk in and right to you, which means I'm not getting much. Instead of just helping me first, you ring up this creepy Mexican with a truckload of alcohol.

CLERK

(heavy sigh)

Ma'am, he was here first, so I serve him first.

WOMAN

Well, I just don't see how-

FISH

(without turning around) I'm not even Mexican.

WOMAN

Excuse me?

FISH

(turns to her and says slowly)

I'm not Mexican.

WOMAN

Well then, wherever you're from, you should go back there.

FISH

It's funny you should say that, because really it should've been me saying that to you.

WOMAN

What the hell does that mean?

FISH

It means: He who inhabits the land of the Buffalo, then tells the Buffalo to go back to his own land, is truly lost.

WOMAN

What? Are you retarded?

FISH

Are you?

The Woman pushes past Fish and addresses the Clerk.

WOMAN

Sir, I need you to remove this man from the store.

CLERK

For what? Asking a question?

WOMAN

He is rude and suspicious and probably illegal. You need to get control of this situation before I call someone who will.

The Woman pulls her phone out and flaunts it. Fish drops his head back and exhales with disappointment.

FISH

(to the Woman)

You think they'll get here fast enough?

WOMAN

Excuse me?

FISH

(slowly)

Do you think the police will get here fast enough?

WOMAN

You know what? I've had it...

She starts dialing 911. Fish sighs and closes his eyes. He's lost his patience.

EXT. GAS STATION - MOMENTS LATER

The sun is peaks out over the skyline and beams on the gas station. Fish exits the station with a deep exhale, a look of disappointment with his bloody hands. One hand filled with bags full of alcohol. After the sun stings his face, he jumps in the tinted car and speeds away.

INT. AIRBNB BEDROOM - DAY

The window blinds are closed and covered with a black sheet. Isla is in bed spooning under the covers with Emma, watching tv. Fish walks in on the two, Emma crying and shaking.

Countless bottles of whiskey lying around the room.

FISH

Isla, what are you doing?

Isla's head pops up.

ISLA

(looking at Fish's bloody hands)

"What did YOU do?" Is a better question.

Fish sits the bags in the bathroom and comes back to the bed.

FISH

Why are you putting her through this, huh?

Fish pulls Emma out from under the covers and Isla tries to pull her back.

ISLA

No! Give her back.

FISH

(serious look) STOP.

Isla looks in his eyes, then quits and rolls back over. Fish walks away with Emma.

FISH (CONT'D)

(to Emma)

And she calls me cruel.

INT. BATHROOM - CONTINUOUS

Fish walks Emma in and sits her in the bathroom on

top of her parents.

FISH

I'll be right back, okay? Just need to talk to my wife a little for a sec. You understand, right?

Emma mumbles.

FISH (CONT'D)

Good.

Fish walks out and closes the door. Emma notices what she's sitting on and screams.

INT. AIRBNB BEDROOM - MOMENTS LATER

Fish walks in and stands in front of the bed.

FISH

Why do you insist on makin' these last few moments harder for her? And where did you even get all these drinks? Did you leave her here alone?

Isla jumps up aggressively and stands in Fish's face.

ISLA

Why do you always pull that "young girls taste the sweetest" shit? Why even give me a chance to disappoint you? To make myself look worthless?

FISH

Disappoint me? Since when have I ever said you look worthless?

ISLA

You didn't have to.

FISH

What's the real problem here? Why don't you just shoot me straight? You jealous of me bringing young girls?

ISLA

NO! You miss it all completely.

FISH

Well then, what is it?

Isla grabs Fish's arm and shows him around the room.

ISLA

You see all these bottles? I can't even get drunk! I don't get periods. I don't age.

FISH

I could see the first thing, but what's wrong with the last two?

ISLA

What's wrong with them? I'm not even a

woman. I’m an animal! Less than that actually. I can't have kids. I can't have a normal family, with a normal life and a normal death one day.

FISH

I mean-

Isla grabs Fish's face.

ISLA

We've personally seen more wars than any person in history. Have you ever really even considered what that means? How many historic events we could personally describe?

Fish doesn't respond.

ISLA (CONT'D)

Does it never get old to you? Does it never make you regret it all?

FISH

I'd never regret this.

ISLA

Yeah? And why's that?

FISH

Because of you.

Isla pauses for a second before laughing hysterically.

ISLA

What?

FISH

Aside from the fact that it wouldn't make sense to regret something I did, and I don't regret the time I got to spend with you. Or at least I didn't.

ISLA

(gets serious)

We're immortal Fish... what could ever make that worth it? It definitely couldn't be me.

FISH

One, we're not immortal. When the world ends, we go with it. And two, YOU agreed to this. I just wanted the woman I loved to not shrivel up and die. I didn't wanna be truly alone forever because any girl I was with had an expiration date. Is it so wrong to love somebody so much that you actually wanna be with them until you die?

ISLA

It's wrong to live like this! We kill and kill and kill, and where does it get us?

Just at a place where now our clocks are reset, but we both know what happens if we don't. How is that supposed to be an ideal life?

Fish sits down on the bed with his head down.

FISH

I just wanted my wife to have my back, and I thought you were willing to do that. Especially since I couldn't control the fact that I ended up like this.

Isla gets closer and lifts his head.

ISLA

You keep calling me your wife, but you didn't see it fit enough to actually marry me.

FISH

Was an eternity together not marriage enough?

ISLA

An eternity as monsters?

FISH

An eternity as lovers.

Isla backs away and looks in the mirror at her reflection.

ISLA

I remember when we couldn't see ourselves in these. When creators were actually craftsmen. That should just be proof that times change and so do the very makeup of things. Including people.

Isla walks to the other side of the room and opens her bag. She pulls out a machete. She walks over to Fish.

ISLA (CONT'D)

Remember what they used to do to vampires? Well, the people they thought were vampires.

Fish stands up.

ISLA (CONT'D)

They'd chop the head off and then burn the body.

Fish's eyes well up.

ISLA (CONT'D)

You could just-

FISH

NO.

He tries to snatch the blade, but Isla pulls away.

ISLA

If you truly loved me, you'd do it.

Fish pauses, his eyes widen with tears falling.

ISLA (CONT'D)

(stern)

If you truly did, you would.

Fish walks closer to her slowly. His breathing is now shaky and harsh. Just close enough to be right over Isla's head. Isla looks up to him with watery eyes and puts the machete between them.

ISLA (CONT'D)

Please?

After a long pause, Isla fixes her mouth to ask again.

DISSOLVE TO:

EXT. AIRBNB - MOMENTS LATER

Fish walks out of the front door and into the street. He looks to the sky and his skin begins to release steam from the sunbeam. He looks at his hands with an existential stare and we drop to a shot of just his lower half. He lifts off the ground and his legs disappear from frame as he floats away.

THE END

The Virtue
of
Relativity

THE VIRTUE OF RELATIVITY

written by

Caleze

What is "TRUTH"?

SUN MOON AND THREE LESS STARS

BLACK SCREEN

SUPER: "CHAPTER I PROTAGONIST - THE GIRL"

INT. THE GIRL'S APARTMENT - HALLWAY - NIGHT

We creep in low through an apartment hallway. Moving closer to an open doorway to a bedroom.

INT. THE GIRL'S APARTMENT - BEDROOM - CONTINUOUS

As we reach the bed, we raise to see THE GIRL (26) lying in bed. She is deep within the covers to a point where only her hair is sticking out. Suddenly, liquid rushes out from under the covers like a flood. It soaks her hair, the entire bed and rushes across the floor in all directions. The Girl rises and gasps, coughing up liquid as she falls out of bed. She lies there, looking around as if she's searching for the nearest help.

INT. THE GIRL'S APARTMENT - LIVING ROOM - DAY

Open close on The Girl's face. She looks tired, ponderous and disengaged with the words of AMANDA (25), who we see as we pull out from The Girl. The Girl is sitting on the sofa, Amanda is sitting on a single seat. Amanda is talking away until she notices The Girl is nowhere near focused on her.

AMANDA

Hey, babe, you good?

Nothing.

AMANDA (CONT'D)

(finger snapping)

Hey!

THE GIRL

(turning with a stunned look)

Oh! Yeah.

AMANDA

Well, I was just telling you about how-

THE GIRL

(looking away)

I had a weird dream last night.

Amanda settles in her chair.

AMANDA

You wanna tell me about it?

THE GIRL

Well...

INSERT: THE GIRL'S DREAM

A dark, wet cave-like place with unearthly sounds and occasional blue pulses radiating through the ground and walls. The Girl continues speaking over the dream in Voiceover, as she does each action in the dream.

THE GIRL (V.O.)

I felt weird already because I was completely naked for whatever reason. I just walked through this cave thing, and it was wet and bumpy. These blue little streams kept shooting through. I kept walking, then I heard these weird sounds. I walked some more, and I stumbled into this kinda room-like area, but it was still the cave.

There were a bunch of black people in the room. I mean, not black people like brown skinned. I mean black like tar black. And they were chanting something that sounded foreign, so I didn't know what it was. And then I looked up and saw this throne with this huge man sitting on it. As soon as I saw him, I just froze and started shaking.

Maybe because he just looked like an oversized silhouette. No face. He uhh... he stood up and walked down the throne to me. His footsteps were so heavy it sounded like an earthquake every time he stepped. When he got to me, he grabbed me by the face with one hand, and I just remember feeling like he was crushing my jaw.

(beat)

INT. THE GIRL'S APARTMENT - LIVING ROOM - DAY

Amanda has her finger over her lip like a professor, waiting for more from The Girl.

AMANDA

Do you remember what happened after that?

The Girl looks to Amanda for half a second, then turns away again as her eyes water.

THE GIRL

I- I uh...

INSERT: THE GIRL'S DREAM

The Girl is lying down belly up on the rocky, wet ground with the giant man on top of her, pressing her head into the ground. He leans in close and screams inaudibly. In return, so does The Girl.

INT. THE GIRL'S APARTMENT - LIVING ROOM - DAY

The Girl looks to Amanda, wiping her tears away.

THE GIRL

Let's just say, it was something I hoped I'd never have happen again.

Amanda pauses a second to think.

AMANDA

Hm... well, based on all the other sessions-

THE GIRL

Please don't call them that.

AMANDA

Okay. During these talks between roommates...

(looks for approval)

The Girl nods.

AMANDA (CONT'D)

You seem to have a lot of dreams that reference that night. Maybe it's time we rethink how we work around that topic.

THE GIRL

What do you mean?

AMANDA

I mean, maybe we should just be straight forward about discussing what happened that night.

The Girl scoffs at Amanda.

THE GIRL

(wound up)

No. I'd really rather not.

AMANDA

Listen, I just think ten years of never really addressing it head on can't be good. It only keeps it boiling until one day you implode from holding it in.

The Girl looks unconvinced.

AMANDA (CONT'D)

Trust me, darling...

(points to her bookshelf with Psych books)

I would know.

The Girl surrenders.

THE GIRL

(crosses arms)

Okay, okay. So, what do you want me to say?

AMANDA

I just want you to detail the events of that night. Where were you? Who was around? Do you remember any random details about that night?

THE GIRL

(shaking and biting her nails)

Well, I uh- I-

Amanda leaves her seat and kneels in front of The Girl, holding her hand.

AMANDA

Honey, [bleep] can't hurt you for saying now.

AMANDA (CONT'D)

He did his time and now he has no idea where you live or work. You're fine here.

THE GIRL

I thought we agreed not to use that name here.

AMANDA

We need to use it now. He no longer holds power over you, and as long as you refuse to say his name, he will. Okay?

THE GIRL

(hesitant) Okay.

AMANDA

Let's kill any lingering piece of him right now. So now we say his name together.

The Girl looks to her eyes widened.

AMANDA (CONT'D)

Come on, girl. We need to do this for you. Right?

The Girl nods and sniffles.

AMANDA (CONT'D)

Okay then, on three.

The Girl nods and sniffles again as she prepares herself.

AMANDA (CONT'D)

Three, two, one-

DISSOLVE TO:

EXT. DOWNTOWN CITY - DAY

A busy downtown street. Cars zip by, homeless people scattered, working people strolling, trendy teens taking pictures in front of buildings and art. The Girl walks out of an apartment building, a leather satchel hanging across her body. A DING in her pocket. She pulls her phone out to see a text notification from "Birth Giver".

BIRTH GIVER (TEXT)

I need you to bring me ibuprofen...

The Girl stops, throws her head back and grunts.

THE GIRL

Come on! Not today.

She walks back to her apartment.

EXT. MOTHER'S HOUSE - DAY

A little, white car pulls into the driveway of a modern-style house. The Girl exits the car with a grocery bag in her hand. She walks to the door, but before knocking, she inhales and exhales with anticipation.

THE GIRL

God, give me strength.

She rings the doorbell. Eventually the door opens and MOTHER (40) is revealed with a cane, shaggy hair and wearing pajamas. The two stand and look at each other up and down awkwardly.

MOTHER

Well, you coming in?

THE GIRL

(exhales) Yeah.

INT. MOTHER'S HOUSE - CONTINUOUS

She steps inside and Mother closes the door behind her. The Girl peers around the house, looking to the many things in disarray.

THE GIRL

(straight-faced)

I love what you've done with the place.

MOTHER

(mockingly)

Ha ha ha! Hilarious. (now serious)

If you would help me out more often, I wouldn't have a messy place.

Ever since your dad you-

THE GIRL

(pointing to Mother)

Don't! You know that's not fair so don't even.

Mother raises her hand and shrugs.

MOTHER

Okay... starting off wonderfully as always.

THE GIRL

Well, if you would just-

The Girl sighs and raises the grocery bag to her mom strictly.

THE GIRL (CONT'D)

Here.

The Mother takes the bag, and The Girl walks into the living room.

MOTHER

Why thanks, dear. (fake smile)

Wherever would I be without you.

INT. MOTHER'S HOUSE - LIVING ROOM - MOMENTS LATER

The Girl walks into the living room and plops down on the suede sofa. Mother wobbles in and she shifts to a deranged look immediately.

MOTHER

Hey! I just had the furniture shampooed and you're sitting all over it. Get up! Get up!

The Girl jumps up and looks to the sofa, which now has a print in it.

MOTHER (CONT'D)

You see! You just ruin everything, you dumb bi-

The Girl scoffs and crosses her arms as if to say, "finish it".

MOTHER (CONT'D)

(calming herself)

I just would like you to be more observant is all, dear.

THE GIRL

Well, where would you have me, Mother?

MOTHER

We should sit on the patio. I could use some sun anyway.

EXT. MOTHER'S HOUSE - PATIO - DAY

Mother and The Girl sit on the patio with drinks - a can of soda for Mother and a water for The Girl - not yet talking. The two trade occasional glances for a while until Mother takes a sip of soda. The Girl shakes her head and looks away.

MOTHER

What?

No response.

MOTHER (CONT'D)

(louder)

What!?

THE GIRL

(never looking to Mother)

Nothing, Mother. Nothing at all.

MOTHER

First of all, what I put into my body is my choice! Okay? My body my choice.

THE GIRL

I'm not sure wanting to drink soda is the right reason to use that phrase.

MOTHER

(finger raised)

Second... second! Second of all, why do

you insist on calling me "Mother"? Why can't you just be normal and call me "Mom"?

THE GIRL

(finally looking to Mother)

Are you not my mother?

MOTHER

That's not the point and you know it.

THE GIRL

Then what is?

MOTHER

The point is "Mother" just sounds so condescending.

(looking away)

It sounds like you're ashamed of me.

The Girl's eyes grow fiery as she whips her body towards Mother.

THE GIRL

Oh, so we're going to talk about "ashamed", huh? Ashamed! Well, let's talk about the fact that you've always been ashamed of me.

MOTHER

That's not true.

THE GIRL

Yes, *Mother*... It is. When I was a little girl, you always treated me like there was no way I could be your daughter because I was nothing like you.

MOTHER

Come on now, that's not fair.

THE GIRL

Yeah, it wasn't fair. Like when Dad brought me to your stupid little party at that event hall, and you made me stay in the restroom the whole time because I didn't "look like your daughter".

MOTHER

A little kid could find a lot to do in a restroom, dear.

THE GIRL

It was four hours!

MOTHER

I told him not to put you in that hideous dress, and had he listened-

THE GIRL

Just-

(waving her hands, eyes shut)

Let's not even discuss it.

The Girl gulps down the rest of her water and turns back to the view. Mother lets her eyes linger on The Girl for a moment before turning back as well. A while passes before they speak again.

THE GIRL (CONT'D)

I had another dream about it last night.

MOTHER

About *it*?

THE GIRL

Yeah.

MOTHER

Well, what was this one like.

THE GIRL

Basically, more dark figures and places. This time I actually saw him.

MOTHER

You saw him?

THE GIRL

Well, not really, but kind of. He was way bigger and black like the others.

MOTHER

Like brown-skinned or just-

THE GIRL

No, black like tar.

MOTHER

Ah okay.

(hesitant)

And did he...

THE GIRL

He started to, but eventually I just woke up and I was wet.

Mother's eyes widen and she tilts her head as she shrugs.

MOTHER

Have you ever considered that these dreams are punishment for lying or kinda shifting the story around?

THE GIRL

What!?

MOTHER

Well, I've never heard of a girl who got raped and got wet after having dreams about it.

THE GIRL

(yelling)

Jeez, what's wrong with you?

MOTHER

I'm just saying-

THE GIRL

See? This is why I hate talking to you. I wasn't wet down there, not just down there. My entire bed was wet like somebody tried to drown me or something.

MOTHER

Well, how is it you think that happened? Because it makes no sense.

THE GIRL

Yeah, I know! And what I don't know is how. It just was. And... why are you just so sure I lied? I know you've never been the type to worry about offending me, but that's a bit far don't you think?

MOTHER

(surrendering)

I think you alone know what happened.

THE GIRL

No, no, no. Don't do that.

MOTHER

Do what?

THE GIRL

Don't just say what I want to hear. You wouldn't do it before, so don't start now.

MOTHER

(sighs)

I'm just saying, you weren't exactly the most trustworthy person back then. That's all.

THE GIRL

So, because I wasn't trustworthy, I deserved to be raped?

MOTHER

Now, hold on. I'm not saying that. What I am saying is: you just might remember it funny. Maybe even needed a little more attention so you tweaked the story some.

THE GIRL

(tears fall)

Who even are you? You're just evil.

MOTHER

(pointing in The Girl's face)

Hey! Don't make it out like you didn't do your share of wrong around here. You lied, you cheated, and you stole! We fought all day every day, and you always seemed like you either wanted more attention or more sorrow from me or your father. And if it weren't for your little story about some guy, who you probably secretly dated prior to it, raping you on the busiest night of the year... your father might still be alive today. Hell, I might not have even had a stroke and ended up some cripple!

The Girl breaks down, tears flowing and her face scrunching tighter by the second. Mother recognizes what she's caused and sits back.

MOTHER (CONT'D)

I don't mean to invalidate you, but I wish you would just see where I'm coming from. Heart problems ran in the family so maybe-

(looking to her shaking hands)

Maybe it would've eventually happened at some point.

No response.

MOTHER (CONT'D)

Come inside when you're ready. I should have some lunch ready.

Mother struggles to her feet with her cane and walks back into the house. The Girl gets into a fetal position on the chair and dries her eyes.

INSERT: THE GIRL'S DREAM

The Girl is falling through the air of a dark pit. She lands in a pool of water and wakes up in her bed at home, falling to the floor in fear.

EXT. MOTHER'S HOUSE - PATIO - DAY

The Girl remains in the fetal position, watching the leaves blow as she lets the few remaining tears dry up.

INT. OFFICE BUILDING - PARKING DECK - DAY

The Girl drives up the levels of the parking deck until she reaches the third floor. She parks and exits the car. When she reaches the door to the Office Building, she pulls a keycard from her leather satchel and scans herself in.

INT. OFFICE BUILDING - HALLWAY - MOMENTS LATER

The Girl walks through the hall and pulls her phone out to text Amanda.

THE GIRL (TEXT)

Which room?

She stops and stands against the wall, waiting for a response. There's a DING from the phone.

AMANDA (TEXT)

Room 406. On the 4th floor today.

The Girl rolls her eyes and responds.

THE GIRL (TEXT)

K.

The girl walks to the elevator and pushes the button. After a while, DING and the doors open, and she steps in.

INT. OFFICE BUILDING - ELEVATOR - CONTINUOUS

Just as she presses floor four, a MAN steps in and looks to the buttons, leaving them as is and stepping to the back, behind The Girl. The Girl begins shaking and holding herself as she tries not to be noticeable. The Man stares at The Girl for a little while. She feels it.

MAN

You were on the wrong floor also?

THE GIRL

(shaky)

Uhh... yeah.

MAN

Yeah, I never can get used to buildings like these, kind of a maze, ya know?

The Girl just smiles and nods.

The elevator reaches the fourth floor and DINGS as the doors slide open and The Girl rushes out.

INT. OFFICE BUILDING - HALLWAY - CONTINUOUS

The Girl walks fast as the Man slowly trails behind her. Just as she disappears around a corner, she begins running until she slams into Amanda, they both fall.

AMANDA

Jeez, you almost took my head off.

THE GIRL

(looking behind her)

I'm sorry, I was scared-

The Man rounds the corner. Seeing the two, he runs up to help.

MAN

Whoa, are you guys okay?

Amanda stands to her feet.

AMANDA

Yeah, Tony. We're good, my friend here just wasn't looking where she was going.

She makes a face at The Girl as she helps her up.

THE GIRL

Sorry.

AMANDA

(pointing to the door down the hall)

Just go on in, Tony. The others are there waiting, and we have some snacks out, so help yourself.

TONY

Alright then.

(waving to The Girl)

Nice to meet you "friend".

Tony walks into the room. The Girl and Amanda wait for the door to close.

THE GIRL

I'm sorry, I thought he was-

AMANDA

It's fine. He's actually a victim who's been coming in recently.

THE GIRL

Ah... got you.

The Girl looks down in embarrassment.

AMANDA

Well, how was your Mom's?

THE GIRL

Same as always.

AMANDA

Meaning she blamed you for everything and insulted you the whole time.

THE GIRL

Yeah.

AMANDA

(grabs The Girl's hand)

I'm sorry about that.

THE GIRL

Thanks.

AMANDA

You have people here who are happy to see you, so cheer up.

AMANDA (CONT'D)

You're about to make some people happy, okay?

The Girl smiles and nods.

AMANDA (CONT'D)

Good.

She puts her arm around the girl and walks her to the room door.

AMANDA (CONT'D)

You all prepared?

THE GIRL

I am.

AMANDA

Great. You'll do just as great as always.

They walk in.

INT. OFFICE BUILDING - MEETING ROOM - CONTINUOUS

A group of about thirty to fifty people are scattered about the room, mingling, eating and getting their note-taking materials together. As Amanda and The Girl walk through, many greet, hug and wave at them as they make their way to a stage and podium at the front of the room. Behind the podium are two chairs and a presentation screen with "Welcome to The Survivors' Convention" on it. The Girl takes a seat and Amanda walks to the podium and adjusts the mic to her.

AMANDA

(into the mic)

If everybody is ready, we can get started now.

Everybody makes their way to their seats. After they're seated Amanda begins to speak.

AMANDA (CONT'D)

Great. How is everyone today?

EVERYONE

Good.

AMANDA

Good, good. I see a lot of new and returning faces, so I'll introduce myself. My name is Amanda Jones, and I am a Sexual Abuse Therapist.

AMANDA (CONT'D)

(motions to The Girl)

My friend and I chose to create a platform for people to not only speak their truth, but to also learn about how to prevent and live life after, sexual abuse. She was actually one of my first patients years ago, and today she's a survivor who is here to present to you guys. I hope you all enjoy and thank you.

Amanda steps away from the podium and everyone claps. The Girl stands and walks to the podium. As they cross each other, Amanda leans into The Girl.

AMANDA (CONT'D)

(whispering)

You got this, girl.

The Girl smiles and nods. As she stands at the podium, looking to the crowd of eager faces, she freezes. Her vision gets cloudy as the vast sea of eyes close in on her. From her seat, Amanda snaps in a sharp whisper.

AMANDA (CONT'D)

(to The Girl)

Hey! You got this.

The Girl looks back to her and nods before closing her eyes and taking a deep breath.

AUDIENCE MEMBER

It's okay, baby! Take your time.

The whole audience joins in clapping and cheering The Girl on as she opens her eyes. The room is light again. She smiles and looks to Amanda who is also clapping. Back to the audience.

THE GIRL

(into the mic)

Hello everyone! So many beautiful faces out there. Today, I would like to talk about-

DISSOLVE TO:

BLACK SCREEN SUPER: "CHAPTER II

PROTAGONIST - THE BOY"

INT. THE BOY'S TRUCK - MORNING

Foggy windows on a truck. THE BOY's (27) truck. He's scrunched into the back seat of the cab, snoring away. His slightly disheveled look matches the fact that he's sleeping in his car. The Boy twitches and jolts until liquid rushes over him like a flood. He rises and gasps for air as he coughs up the liquid that's now streaming from the truck doors. He lies there, looking around as if he's searching for the nearest help.

EXT. WINDY RIVER CINEMA AND TAPHOUSE - DAY

The Boy's truck pulls into the lot of a movie theater - Windy River Cinema and Taphouse - being renovated inside and out.

He parks in a space and steps out of the truck wearing construction gear and eating a granola bar. The Boy walks with a noticeable limp. He looks to his watch, it's 7:56 A.M. Others either arrive in groups or merge into them as they enter the building. The Boy is walking alone. He's used to it.

INT. WINDY RIVER CINEMA AND TAPHOUSE - LOBBY - MONTAGE

- The Boy on a ladder drilling in a giant decorative piece.
- Workers carry floor tiles. MONTAGE CONTD.

- The Boy and another worker measure out counters and cabinets.
- All workers taking lunch break outside.
- The Boy in a group, ripping up the old floor tiles.
- The Boy looks to his watch, it's 2:12 P.M.

EXT. WINDY RIVER CINEMA AND TAPHOUSE - MOMENTS LATER

The Boy runs out of the front door and over to BILL (54), his manager, who's reading a clipboard beside the building.

THE BOY

Hey, Bill.

BILL

(eyes on the clipboard) Yeah.

THE BOY

I've gotta see my P.O. at three. Or- Well... I guess my counselor.

Bill says nothing for a second while he continues reading his clipboard. Finally, he looks to The Boy, then his watch, then back to The Boy.

BILL

Alright.

He looks back down to his clipboard.

THE BOY

(straight-faced) Thanks.

The Boy walks to his truck and drives off.

INT. ASSAULT COUNSELING BUILDING - HALLWAY - DAY

The Boy comes through the front door of the Probation Office Building. The building has a modern office look to it, with plants, art, and pictures of animals. He walks to a door with a tag printed "DR. SARAH KERSEY". The Boy knocks on the door.

DR. KERSEY (O.S.)

Come in!

INT. ASSAULT COUNSELING BUILDING - KERSEY'S OFFICE - CONT.

The Boy walks into a very neatly organized office. Every piece of furniture is white except for the patient's seat, which is black. The only color resides in decoration. Dr. Kersey's desk looks like one out of a furnishing catalogue in that it's perfectly organized symmetrically. Dr. Kersey looks like a young and semi-attractive schoolteacher. She stands to greet The Boy.

DR. KERSEY

(smiling)

Hello, thanks for coming...

She notices his limp.

THE BOY

Hey.

They shake hands.

DR. KERSEY

And being here on time.

They both look to the clock on the wall, it's 3:05.

THE BOY

Sorry about that. I-

DR. KERSEY

(walking back to her desk) No problem, no problem. I understand it's our first time meeting and that allows for a little leeway.

She cracks a half smile while standing behind her desk. The Boy has a hesitant look.

DR. KERSEY (CONT'D)

Would you like to sit?

THE BOY

(he sits)

Yeah.

Dr. Kersey sits and goes through a stack of stapled

papers.

DR. KERSEY

(looking at papers)

So, I see here that you were convicted of rape just about nine years ago. You did eight and a half of fifteen possible years due to good behavior.

She looks to The Boy, he nods.

DR. KERSEY (CONT'D)

(back to papers)

I also see that you work for Lamen and Guild Construction. There for the past few months.

(to The Boy)

How is it you got into construction so easily? Don't you need training or vocational school for it?

THE BOY

While I was in prison, they had me in a lot of work programs.

DR. KERSEY

Work programs, huh? How was that?

THE BOY

Once you can get passed it basically being slave labor, it's okay.

Dr. Kersey gives a prolonged, unreadable look as she nods her head. She looks into his eyes as they're glossy, then looks back down.

DR. KERSEY

(back to papers)

Hmm. So, maybe we'll take a little break from the file and just do some typical questions you would've done with your P.O.-

THE BOY

If you don't mind, what exactly is this? Like I get that you're an Assault Counselor, but what is it exactly we're doing here.

She gives another prolonged, unreadable look, no head nod.

DR. KERSEY

Yeah, so we're here basically to get into your psyche now that you're back in normal life. Myself being a former therapist, we want to see exactly how far you've come, if at all, and if you're ready to stay out here among civilians or not.

THE BOY

Right.

DR. KERSEY

Understood?

THE BOY

Yeah.

DR. KERSEY

Okay. Now, to the questions. Any contact with law enforcement recently?

THE BOY

(sighs)

No.

DR. KERSEY

Any drugs or alcohol?

THE BOY

No.

DR. KERSEY

(calm tone)

Any drugs or alcohol?

The Boy looks at her in confusion.

THE BOY

No.

DR. KERSEY

(still serious)

Any drugs or alcohol?

The Boy gives a crazy look as his leg jolts. He exhales deeply.

THE BOY

I already said NO.

DR. KERSEY

So why are your eyes a little glossy?

THE BOY

I just don't get good sleep. Haven't since I was inside. Bad dreams now, I guess.

DR. KERSEY

Like fever dreams? Maybe from a little substance abuse?

THE BOY

No! No substance abuse! I already-

DR. KERSEY

(annoyingly calm)

No need to get angry. Just doing my due diligence.

The Boy sits back to gather himself. Dr Kersey

watches.

DR. KERSEY (CONT'D)

Maybe tell me about one of these dreams.

No response.

DR. KERSEY (CONT'D)

Maybe the one from last night. Assuming that's why you look so tired.

The Boy glances at her, seeing she's serious.

THE BOY

(thinking)

I uh- I was in a cave...

INSERT: THE BOY'S DREAM

A dark, wet cave-like place with unearthly sounds and occasional blue pulses radiating through the ground and walls. The Boy continues speaking over the dream in voice-over, as he does each action in the dream.

THE BOY (V.O.)

I was completely naked. I mean, completely naked. The ground was rocky and wet, so it was super uncomfortable. I walked further into the cave and stumbled into this room full of black people.

INT. ASSAULT COUNSELING BUILDING - KERSEY'S OFFICE - DAY

Dr. Kersey frowns and tilts her head.

THE BOY

(pointing down)

Black like this chair black.

DR. KERSEY

(understanding)

Ah. Okay.

INSERT: THE BOY'S DREAM

The Boy is standing is the room surrounded by people.

THE BOY (V.O.)

They were all chanting, kinda angry-like. I walked in some more, and a group of them were holding on to this Dark Woman. She was crying and flailing around. She looked up at me and then screamed so loud my ears started bleeding.

(MORE)

THE BOY (V.O.) (CONT'D)

After that, she just pointed at me, and these shackles wrapped around my hands and feet. Then, the crowd of people just started beating me. Punchin' and kickin', punchin' and kickin'. I just remember feeling like they were gonna crush me, but they never did. I was always just okay enough to live through it.

INT. ASSAULT COUNSELING BUILDING - KERSEY'S OFFICE - DAY

Dr. Kersey's face is still unreadable.

DR. KERSEY

Anything else?

THE BOY

Well, I also woke up wet.

DR. KERSEY

Like you peed on yourself?

THE BOY

No, like I had a bucket of water just thrown on me. Or at least something like water. It had a slightly different feeling.

DR. KERSEY

So, you're saying it followed you out of the dream.

THE BOY

No. Well... maybe. I don't really know. I *just* remember my truck was soaked and the liquid was rushing out of the doors.

DR. KERSEY

Your truck?

THE BOY

Yeah, I uh... sleep in my truck.

DR. KERSEY

(nods)

Mhm.

(beat)

So, what do you think the dream meant?

THE BOY

I often have dreams about my case, prison, losing my family. Maybe it's about that.

DR. KERSEY

Do you think you deserved those things?

THE BOY

The stuff from my case?

DR. KERSEY

Yes.

THE BOY

Of course not. I've always said I was innocent.

DR. KERSEY

But doesn't everybody?

THE BOY

Well, yeah but not when they've already done the time. What would be the point in going through what I've gone through just to keep lying?

DR. KERSEY

So, you believe it was unfair that you were found guilty?

THE BOY

Yeah, it was. They never even had evidence that she was telling the truth.

DR. KERSEY

There was also no evidence that you weren't telling a lie.

They trade stares for a while.

THE BOY

I mean, sure but-

DR. KERSEY

It's also well documented that you had a violent past prior to this case.

THE BOY

Yeah but-

Dr. Kersey flips open some pages and keeps going.

DR. KERSEY

It says here that prior to the case, you had been charged with Battery. You were young so you got off with community service, but it was enough to cast doubt on what you had to say about this.

THE BOY

I was a kid then.

DR. KERSEY

Yes, but also a kid who went from violence to sexual violence. I'm sure with your stent in prison, you know that seems like a possible natural escalation if implied. Would you agree?

The Boy's eye twitches as his leg goes back to jolting.

DR. KERSEY (CONT'D)

Maybe even then you could see how nobody would bat an eye when you complained about the many things that happened to you in prison.

Including, but definitely not limited to that hip fracture of yours.

The Boy is shaking, his face turning, his eyes fiery. Dr. Kersey sits with a blank face still, never flinching.

EXT. ASSAULT COUNSELING BUILDING - FRONT DOOR - DAY

The Boy rushes out of the building and stops on the sidewalk. He's almost hyperventilating as he gathers himself. He puts his hands on his hips and grunts as he looks to the sky.

INT. WINDY RIVER CINEMA AND TAPHOUSE - LOBBY - MONTAGE

- The Boy driving nails.
- Workers installing machines.
- Lunch break outside.
- The Boy hammering, look to his watch: 12:32 P.M.

EXT. PIZZA RESTAURANT - NIGHT

The Boy walks into the lot of a Pizza Restaurant, still wearing his construction gear and holding a bag. He enters the restaurant.

INT. PIZZA RESTAURANT - HOST STAND - CONTINUOUS

The Boy walks in the door and scans the room. A bar, an open kitchen, people laughing and talking with their families and friends, the empty host stand in front of him. For a while he stands alone until a beautiful girl - SOPHIA (24) - in all black walks to the host stand.

SOPHIA

(with a bright smile)

Hey, welcome in. What can I help you with?

The Boy is struck by her looks but tries to maintain his composure.

THE BOY

I wanna order something. To go. What would you recommend?

SOPHIA

(thinks)

Well, let's see. It might sound weird, but the subs are great.

THE BOY

Subs from a pizza joint, huh?

They both laugh.

SOPHIA

Yeah, I told you it might sound weird. But if it's just you, the subs are a great size and they're all really good.

Sophia slides a menu across the desk to The Boy.

THE BOY

Hmm, how 'bout this. You just pick one and I'll eat that.

SOPHIA

(smiling)

You sure?

THE BOY

Yeah. You look trustworthy enough.

They trade smiles while Sophia looks over the menu. She picked one.

SOPHIA

Got it! That'll be six-fifty.

The Boy nods and goes into his wallet, handing her his debit card. He stares at her soft hands, flowing hair and perfect little face. TRACY, a waitress, is cleaning a table as she stares at The Boy. When they make eye contact, Tracy quickly walks to the back. Sophia finishes and hands the card and receipt back to The Boy.

SOPHIA (CONT'D)

Alright then, would you like anything to drink while you wait?

THE BOY

Uhh… no thanks. I'm good.

Sophia takes a second to look him up and down.

SOPHIA

So, you're a construction worker?

THE BOY

Uh, yeah. I'm working on that theater ummm... Windy River or something like that.

SOPHIA

Oh, the one with Taphouse at the end, right?

THE BOY

Yeah, that one.

SOPHIA

What does that even mean anyway?

THE BOY

Hey, I wish you could tell me.

They both laugh.

THE BOY (CONT'D)

I actually walked here from there. My truck broke down and I'll probably need a new one.

SOPHIA

Ah, that sucks. Does construction pay well enough to replace it right now?

(realizing what she said)

If you don't mind me asking. I'm sorry, I-

THE BOY

It's fine. No problem. It does if you do it for a while, I haven't been at it very long, so I'm playing "catchup".

SOPHIA

Makes sense.

THE BOY

The Mexicans are so ahead of us though, we should get on their level.

Sophia chuckles and opens her mouth like "no you didn't"?

SOPHIA

What does that mean?

THE BOY

(leans in)

I mean: They come and all drive one truck to work every day. Might be six to ten of them in some old F-150, but they're getting that work done. Then, as time goes on, they take turns buying each individual a truck in order. That way after working long enough, they all have trucks and more room for others to repeat the process.

SOPHIA

Wow, that's actually really smart.

THE BOY

It is. But I guess that's why they make up the majority of the industry.

SOPHIA

(smiling)

I guess so, huh?

TRACY walks up to the counter with a bag. Sophia takes it from her.

SOPHIA (CONT'D)

Thanks, Tracy.

TRACY

Of course.

Tracy looks to The Boy again, then quickly walks away.

SOPHIA

(handing bag to The Boy)

Here ya go. I really hope you enjoy.

The Boy takes the bag.

THE BOY

(smiling)

Thanks a bunch.

He almost walks out, but he comes back.

THE BOY (CONT'D)

Hey, my name's [bleep] by the way.

SOPHIA

Hey, I'm Sophia.

THE BOY

You ought to give me your number so I can tell you whether I like it or not.

Sophia's face lights up.

SOPHIA

Of course!

The Boy pulls out a flip phone.

THE BOY

I hope you don't mind. I'm kinda old school I guess.

SOPHIA

Of course not.

(takes the phone)

No problem.

Sophia types the number in and hands the phone back.

THE BOY

Great. I'll be letting you know soon.

SOPHIA

I hope so. have a great one.

THE BOY

Take it easy.

He exits the restaurant. Sophia steps back and blushes. Tracy approaches her.

TRACY

You two look friendly.

SOPHIA

Yeah, he's cute, right? Really different, I guess.

TRACY

Oh he's "different" alright.

SOPHIA

What?

TRACY

I couldn't figure out where I knew him from, college or something.

Then it hit me: He was that guy that raped some

girl some years ago.

SOPHIA

No!

TRACY

Yeah. It was almost a decade ago, but he did some years for it. I guess he got out early.

Sophia leans against the counter staring out to The Boy drive off.

TRACY (CONT'D)

I just figured you should know.

Tracy walks away. Sophia drops her head and walks away as well.

EXT. WINDY RIVER CINEMA AND TAPHOUSE - DAY

The Boy sits outside of the movie theater, on the curb, eating a protein bar. He looks at his watch, it's 12:15 P.M. The Boy whips out his phone and dials Sophia. His little buttons beeping with every touch. The line connects.

SOPHIA (V.O.)

Hello?

THE BOY

Hey there! It's [bleep], the construction worker from last night.

SOPHIA (V.O.)

Oh... yeah.

THE BOY

I was calling to make sure I-

SOPHIA (V.O.)

Why didn't you just tell me?

THE BOY

(beat)

Tell you what?

SOPHIA (V.O.)

Tell me you're a convicted rapist!

THE BOY

That I'm- Sophia-

SOPHIA (V.O.)

How do I know you weren't just trying to lure me out to be your next victim, huh?

THE BOY

Whoa! I didn't even- I got convicted, but I didn't even do it. They just buried me.

SOPHIA (V.O.)

How does that even-

THE BOY

I just- I don't see how it makes sense to tell you: "Hey, how's it going? By the way, I was convicted of rape, but I really didn't do it. Trust me!"

SOPHIA (V.O.)

You were supposed to be honest! I wasted my time last night thinking I found somebody worth my time, but instead it was just *you*.

THE BOY

Wasted your time? On me?

SOPHIA (V.O.)

Have a nice life, and don't come back to the restaurant. I've already told management about you. Goodbye, [bleep].

Sophia hangs up. The Boy stands there shocked as he drops his phone to his side. He looks around, then up to the sky.

EXT. WINDY RIVER CINEMA AND TAPHOUSE - NIGHT

The Boy walks from up the street, into the parking lot of the movie theater. He reaches his truck and gets into the front cab.

INT. THE BOY'S TRUCK - CONTINUOUS

The backseat still moist, he sits in the front and

lays the seat back. He folds his arms and stares out to the stars. His eyes slowly close as he drifts away.

DISSOLVE TO:

BLACK SCREEN SUPER: "CHAPTER III

PROTAGONIST - THE TRUTH"

INT. THE GIRL'S APARTMENT - BEDROOM - NIGHT

The Girl is in bed sleeping, curled up under a new set of blankets.

INT. THE BOY'S TRUCK - NIGHT

The Boy is in the front seat of his truck, sleeping away with his arms folded.

INTERCUT THE GIRL AND THE BOY

The Girl twitches and begins shaking. Her eyes roll back. The Boy twitches and begins shaking. His eyes roll back. The Girl's covers fly off as her body stiffens like a plank.

The Boy's arms unfold as he stiffens like a plank.

INT. THE CAVE - DREAM

The Girl and The Boy fall into a dark pit together (SLO-MO). Both completely naked. They land in a body of blue liquid and struggle to get back to the surface. Frantically staying afloat, they notice each other. They trade confused looks, until they are sucked down to the bottom of the liquid and sucked through a wavy, oval-shaped, portal at the bottom.

They come out of another oval-shaped, portal sitting on a wall vertically. When they fall out, they land against each other on a rocky surface. A spotlight seemingly on them, they stand.

A group of the Black-Colored People come out of the shadows and into the shrinking spotlight. As the creatures touch the light, it burns them. The pair stand back-to-back as their operating space shrinks until they are flush against each other. The Boy and Girl scream and fight as the creatures swallow them up, the light going with them.

INT. THE GIRL'S APARTMENT - BEDROOM - NIGHT

The Girl falls from above, now naked, into her bed as water rushes down with her.

EXT. THE BOY'S TRUCK - NIGHT

The Boy falls from above, now naked, into the bed of his truck as water rushes down with him.

INTERCUT THE GIRL AND THE BOY

The Girl falls off the bed, to the floor, throwing up liquid.

The Boy throws his head over the side of the truck, throwing up liquid.

The Girl covers herself with her arms and rocks back and forth in the fetal position.

The Boy falls back into the truck, lying on his side, in the fetal position.

INT. THE GIRL'S APARTMENT - KITCHEN - DAY

The Girl and Amanda are in the middle of a heated discussion. Amanda cleaning and The Girl following her around.

THE GIRL

I need to do this! Once and for all! I just wanna know that I'm not crazy.

AMANDA

(cleaning a dish)

You'rc not! At least you won't be if you don't do this.

THE GIRL

I. HAVE. TO.

AMANDA

(stops cleaning)

But you don't. You had a bad dream and now you just wanna-

THE GIRL

He was there. He was in it. We didn't talk but, I knew he was conscious. He knew I was there too.

AMANDA

Listen to yourself.

(grabs The Girl's hand)

I just want you to be safe. As your friend. And as your counselor, I want you to consider that it is against the law for him to make contact with you. Text, call, in person... it's all bad.

THE GIRL

I have to. I have to get clarity. This is the only way.

AMANDA

But it's not.

THE GIRL

He did almost nine years for me, the least I could do is talk this out with him. The dream, the case, everything.

Amanda leans against the counter and sighs. The Girl puts her hand on Amanda's shoulder.

THE GIRL (CONT'D)

I have to do this, Amanda. I won't get past it if I don't.

AMANDA

(beat)

At least tell me you have a set plan.

THE GIRL

I do.

AMANDA

In a public place.

THE GIRL

Yes.

AMANDA

Okay. You want me to tag along?

THE GIRL

No, I need to do this alone. I have to find the truth.

The girls hug.

INT. WINDY RIVER CINEMA AND TAPHOUSE - BATHROOM - DAY

The Boy stands in the bathroom, looking into the mirror. He turns on the faucet and throws some water over his face. He dries that off with paper towels, then back to the mirror.

THE BOY

You've gotta do this, man. You've lived with this long enough. It's time for y'all to just get the truth out there no matter what.

Even if it means you could go back to jail. It's gotta be worth it.

She deserves it and so do you. All the finger-pointing all the lying, ya'll have to get it together after all this. You're seeing her in your dreams, man. That's no bueno, man. You gotta find the truth. You gotta-

A construction worker walks in and passes The Boy with a judging look. The Boy nods to him - the worker just turns his head and walks into a stall.

THE BOY (CONT'D)

(back to the mirror)

You got this.

(deep breathe)

The Boy exits the restroom.

EXT. CAFE - DAY

The Girl walks up to the Cafe window and peers in. She clutches her stomach and moves to stand against the wall. She inhales and exhales deeply, then goes in.

INT. CAFE - CONTINUOUS

Arms crossed, The Girl slowly walks through the lively cafe. Study groups, business meetings, lone workers, coffee enthusiasts - the place is pretty busy. She walks to the ordering counter.

EXT. CAFE - DAY

The Boy walks up to the Cafe door and hesitates as he holds the door handle. A couple walks up and stops. He looks back, noticing them. The Boy half smiles and opens the door for them. The couple smiles and nods on their way in, but The Boy stands at the door for a while, thinking, before inhaling and exhaling on his way in.

INT. CAFE - CONTINUOUS

The Boy walks in, seeing The Girl at a table waiting. She looks up and they lock eyes as he walks in (SLO-MO). He sits in front of her as they both shake. They stare deep into each other's eyes as they water. Neither can speak yet. They just stare.

CUT TO BLACK.

THE END

T&F 69

www.ingramcontent.com/pod-product-compliance
Lightning Source LLC
LaVergne TN
LVHW010659110826
845149LV00014B/3174

* 9 7 8 0 9 9 7 7 8 0 4 7 5 *